DANGEROUS PRINCESS

RETRIBUTION GAMES BOOK 6

ELLA MILES

Copyright © 2021 by Ella Miles

EllaMiles.com

Ella@ellamiles.com

Cover design © CBC Designs / Designs by Daqri

All rights reserved.

No part of this book may be reproduced in any form or by any electronic or mechanical means, including information storage and retrieval systems, without written permission from the author, except for the use of brief quotations in a book review.

RETRIBUTION GAMES SERIES

Mistaken Hero
Forbidden Princess
Tempted Hero
Fatal Princess
Tortured Hero
Dangerous Princess

1
BECKETT

Did I win because I was the one who impregnated her? Or did I win because I won her heart?

I can't wait to ask her those and a million other questions after the wedding. She's mine, and together we will conquer the world.

Ri and her father reach the end of the aisle, and I hold out my arm for Ri to take it.

Corsi looks at me. "Protect Rialta with your life."

"I swear I will," I vow.

He nods and then passes Ri's hand from his arm to mine. Together, she and I take two steps toward the minister.

"Can I lift your veil? I want to look you in the eyes when I marry you," I ask her.

She nods.

Slowly, I lift her veil, careful not to mess up her hair or makeup. I'm expecting to see Ri's beautiful big eyes staring back at me with a teasing gaze, but that's not what I get. In fact, Ri isn't the one staring back at me at all—it's the woman I helped Ri save.

I blink in disbelief. This has to be a mistake.

"Who are you?" I ask.

"Rialta Corsi," she replies.

I must have heard her wrong. This can't be the truth. This woman isn't Rialta.

No—my Rialta is taller, has darker hair, a fierce sparkle in her brown eyes. My Rialta's arms are toned and ready to beat any man in this room. My Rialta looks at me with love and lust with an undercurrent of hatred.

This woman is an imposter. She's a similar height but at least an inch shorter. She has dark hair like Rialta, but it's lighter with auburn highlights. There is no fierceness in her eyes. Her arms look like chicken wings—thin and scrawny, nowhere near ready to fight. And this woman looks at me with indifference. There's no emotion at all in her eyes when she sees me.

The woman standing before me was made to wear this dress with her model-thin frame. With a tiara in her hair, she looks like a fairytale princess—not the princess warrior I've come to know.

I blink several times, thinking this has to be a mistake. I have to be hallucinating this person. Maybe I'm hallucinating because I can't believe I'll ever actually get to marry Rialta. I don't deserve her, and my dreams will never come true.

But every time I blink, this imposter is still standing in front of me.

My mouth falls open, and I swear my heart stops. I can't breathe. I can't think. This can't be happening—not after everything. I can't go from being married to a woman I hate to a woman I don't even know, not while the woman I love walks this earth.

The imposter doesn't speak, neither do I.

We stare at each other in a desperate search for answers. I'm not sure either of us has a clue as to what is going on.

I don't know how I muster it or even where it comes from, but I finally get words out. "I don't understand."

She sucks in a breath but doesn't speak. I can see the hesitation in her eyes, along with fear and concern. She doesn't understand either.

I look around the church, looking for the real Rialta, for Ri. As I quickly search the pews, the aisle, the banisters, the stage behind us, I find her nowhere. She's not here.

I look to the three men standing behind me as my best men—Hayes, Lennox, and Gage. They finally get a full look at her face and seem just as shocked as me. None of them say anything. It will take them some time to process this before they can be helpful, so I'm on my own.

I look to Corsi sitting in the first pew on Rialta's side, and he returns my gaze with stern eyes. Then I see the gun he has laid out casually on his lap.

We all have guns. It's four against one, so I don't know what he thinks he's going to accomplish with that threat.

Corsi looks to the minister and nods his head.

The minister begins speaking, but I don't hear any of his words—I can't. I keep looking at Rialta, urgently trying to process everything.

What am I missing?

Did the real Ri try to warn me?

Did she give me some clue?

Is she in danger? Is she dead, and this woman was hired to take her place as a shitty impersonation?

"Where is the real Ri?" I ask her.

She blinks at me but doesn't even bother to open her

mouth and offer me an explanation. I assume it's because of Corsi. She's as terrified of him as everyone else in this city.

What do I do?

I need answers. I need to know what happened to Ri. That's all that matters right now. I need to stop thinking of myself and save her. If I can't get answers from this woman, then I need to try Corsi.

I don't care if I start a war with him. A war has already been started.

I'll do anything for Ri. I'll do anything to protect her. If I have to die to keep her safe, then so be it.

I take a step toward Corsi before I hear Lennox shout, "Beckett, don't move!"

I stop, confused as to what he's seeing. But as I turn in his direction—a flicker of red light on my chest catches my eyes.

I stare down at the red dot—a threat to stay put. To get married to a complete stranger. To do as Corsi wants.

I quickly glance around the church, trying to find the person who has me in the crosshairs of their sniper rifle. I don't see anyone, but the red dot doesn't move, so neither do I.

I look to Corsi, and he raises his eyebrows at me in a challenge.

"I'm not going to marry her. This wasn't the deal. I was to marry Ri, not this imposter," I say, cutting off the minister and not looking at the woman in the wedding dress next to me. I don't know if I've offended her by saying I won't marry her, but I really could care less about her opinion right now. All I care about is finding out what happened to Ri.

"Actually, the deal was that if you win, you get to marry

my daughter—Rialta Corsi. You get to produce an heir with my daughter, and my kingdom is yours. That was the deal."

"This isn't Rialta Corsi!" I protest.

Corsi only gives me a sly smile. I've been betrayed. Somehow everything I've believed turned out to be false.

"Beckett Monroe, let me introduce you to Rialta Corsi, my daughter," Corsi says.

My eyes cut to the woman in front of me, and I see moisture welling in the corner of her eyes. She's about to cry. She looks the same age as Ri but somehow feels decades younger. She's timid where if Ri were here, she'd be outspoken, demanding what she wants from the room.

"Where is Ri?" I ask through gritted teeth. My hand fists as I consider my options to stop this.

"It doesn't matter where she is. What matters is that you won. You won the games; now you have to accept the reward. Marry my daughter and fulfill the contract you entered into when you started the games."

"I won't be marrying anyone today."

Another red dot appears on my chest, followed by a third.

I look Corsi straight in the eyes—leader to leader.

"Marry her, or you die," Corsi says simply.

"You won't kill me. If you do, you won't have anyone left to marry your daughter. You obviously need someone to marry your daughter very badly. Why? I don't know or care, but you need me. You won't kill me."

Corsi frowns, but the dots don't leave my chest. He studies me carefully, thinking of another way to manipulate me.

"Fine, you leave me no choice. If you don't marry my daughter, then I'll kill Ri," he says.

My eyes widen, and a knot forms deep in my stomach. "You wouldn't. I don't know who she is to you, but you care about her."

"I'm a cruel man, Beckett. You know this. It's why I'm the leader that I am. Leaders in this world have to do some pretty horrible things. You've killed men that didn't exactly deserve it for the greater good. This would be no different. Ri knows her place. She would willingly die if it ensured your marriage to Rialta."

"Ri wants this?" I say in words barely audible. I can't believe it.

"Let me talk to Ri," I plead, needing to hear it from her lips. I need to understand what I'm not understanding.

"No," Corsi says flatly.

I glare at him. "If you want me to consider marrying Rialta, then let me talk to Ri." It's the most ridiculous thing I've ever said. I still can't believe I'm talking about two different people, that Rialta and Ri aren't the same person.

"No, you'll marry my daughter. If you don't, then Ri dies. Simple as that. You don't get to talk to anyone. You don't get to talk to Ri. You'll do what I say, or she dies," Corsi dictates.

My heart stops cold at the thought of Ri dying, but he's at least confirmed to me that she's alive—I think.

"How do I know Ri's even alive? How do I know you haven't already killed her?" I ask.

Corsi narrows his eyes at me. He doesn't like being challenged. He doesn't like that I'm pushing back.

"Rialta, would you like to confirm that Ri is still alive?" Corsi asks her.

I turn toward her, looking her dead in the eyes. She's

much easier to read than Corsi or Ri, so I'll be able to tell if she's lying.

Rialta doesn't meet my gaze initially. She stares down at the floor as her bottom lip trembles just slightly.

Please, God, please let her be alive.

"Rialta, please," I whisper in a prayer.

She finally looks up at me. I don't know what she sees when she looks me in the eyes. I don't know if whatever she sees is the reason she finally gives me an answer.

"Ri—she's alive," she says in the softest voice. I stare at her closely. Her eyes are sincere. Her voice is honest. She told the truth. Ri's alive.

"But she won't be if you don't marry her," Corsi barks.

I swallow down the lump in my throat. I just got out of one loveless marriage, and now I'm about to be locked in another. I was the leader of the Retribution Kings, but I'm sure that became void the second my marriage to Odette was annulled.

If I marry Rialta and she produces an heir, I become the leader of the Corsi's mafia—an even stronger group. At least I will no longer be at direct war with my brother and his family. And after I marry Rialta, Corsi will start grooming me to take over. I'll have resources to help my family.

But can I go through with another fake marriage?

No, I can't.

I look down at the dots on my chest. I don't have a choice but to marry Rialta, this imposter. I'll die if I don't. Ri will die if I don't.

I turn back to the minister and hold out my arm to Rialta. Marriage doesn't mean anything. It's just a contract I can dissolve later. I just need to stay alive and keep Ri alive. I'll figure out how to get out of the marriage later.

I don't glance at her, but I feel Rialta take my arm, and we step up to the minister, who looks in Corsi's direction. Corsi must nod at him to continue because the minister resumes speaking, and this time, I listen.

The minister is brief in his opening remarks, quickly getting to the vows part. I feel uneasiness in waves coming off Lennox, Gage, and Hayes. I don't have to look at them to know they all have their hands on their guns, ready for a fight to break out at a moment's notice.

The red dots are gone from my chest, but I'm sure they're on my back. They won't shoot me dead, but they won't let me walk out of here either without finishing this ceremony.

"Do you, Rialta Corsi, take Beckett Monroe to be your husband?" the minister looks to Rialta.

I look straight ahead, giving Rialta space to answer the question. It feels far too intimate to look her in the eyes.

I wait for her to say 'I do,' but if she said the words, I didn't hear it. Although maybe I didn't want to hear it. If she said 'I do,' then I'll have to go next, and it's going to kill me to say it, even if it's the only way to keep Ri alive.

But she must not have said anything because the minister keeps looking at her in earnest, waiting for her to say the magic words.

Finally, I look over at Rialta, wondering why she hasn't spoken. I'm a complete stranger to her, but I expect she wants this since she walked down the aisle willingly.

When I look at her, I see a scared woman. Her face is white, her bottom lip is trembling, and her throat is tightened. There is no way she will be able to speak; she's in too much shock.

I don't know how to help her. I don't even know if she is truly Rialta or what Corsi's endgame is. I don't know why this marriage is being forced. I don't understand any of it.

"Purse your lips and try to breathe," I try to encourage her, just hoping the woman will calm down and not have a full-blown panic attack. Although, maybe a panic attack will help me stall to figure a way out of this wedding.

She purses her lips like I told her and is about to breathe when I feel her swaying.

"Rialta, are you okay?" I ask, but she can't answer.

She's falling.

Her grip on my arm releases as she falls back. I barely have time to reach behind her head and cradle it to keep her skull from hitting the hard stone.

I don't know what just happened. *Was she shot? Did she faint to avoid marrying me?* I don't know. What I do know is that whatever happened, I've been spared my worst nightmare—at least temporarily.

I won't let the chance go to waste.

2

RI

I'M HIDING in the shadows of the rafters when Beckett and the guys walk into the church. I wasn't sure they would show or if Beckett would realize he's about to get married. The fact that he showed up in a suit tells me he knows exactly what he's in for.

Well, not exactly. He doesn't know the whole truth—far from it. But I have no doubt that by the end of the night, he'll be married. The plan will go off smoothly, but not without my heart breaking.

I'll be surprised if everyone in the church doesn't hear my heart shatter into a million pieces and fall all over the floor when Beckett says, 'I do.' But it is my duty to arrange this. It is my honor. My job. My life. And I will do it without shedding a tear.

But when I go home tonight, there will be floods of tears. I'll cry uncontrollably without being able to stop, but not now. Now I have a job to do.

I watch as Beckett happily walks down the aisle with the others. I don't know how to feel about his attitude. *Would he really have been that happy to marry me? Or did he really just want Vincent's power and the ability to stop the war against his brother?*

I don't allow myself to think too hard about the answers. The answers don't matter. What matters is getting them married, getting her safe.

Beckett waits with his men at the end of the aisle, and the church doors open a moment later. Vincent and Rialta start walking down the aisle. She's beautiful in her fluffy dress, complete with tiara. It's not my style, but it suits her.

How long will it take Beckett to realize I'm not the woman in that dress?

I get my answer seconds later when Beckett lifts her veil. I told her not to let him do that. I told her not to speak, wait as long as possible. But of course, he realized something was off the second she got near him.

I expect the shock on Beckett's face. What I don't expect is the rest of his emotions. In addition to shock, there's disappointment, fear, and brokenness. There's something else too, something I dare not name—not now. It doesn't matter anymore. It's all done, or it's about to be.

But the question sneaks into my head—*did I make the right choice?*

I'm in a haze of feelings when Beckett takes a step toward Vincent, and I automatically aim my rifle's laser at his chest. I would never shoot him, not unless he was threatening her life. But the threat alone will keep him in place long enough for Vincent to convince him he has no choice but to stay.

Lennox yells out, and Beckett notices the red dot on his chest. Beckett looks in my direction, trying to find his assailant. He can't see me—I'm too well hidden in the shadows. But for a second, I think he knows it's me. We can always feel each other. We can always sense when each other is near. I have no doubt he feels my presence as I always feel his.

Hopefully, those feelings go away soon enough. We will be living too close together to be feeling such things for the rest of our lives. I hold my breath, remaining as still as possible until Beckett finally looks away.

Beckett talks to Vincent. I barely listen. I focus on keeping the laser pointed at his chest. I'm not the only one up here. I might be Rialta's main protection, but on a night like tonight, we have a full army protecting her.

I look to the three men standing to Beckett's right. All of them have hands buried beneath their jackets, most likely gripping a gun should a battle break out. Their eyes circle around the room, looking for the threat. They know we're up here in the church rafters, but they can't see us. What they can see is Rialta—and they look at her like she's the enemy.

I sigh. It's going to take a while for them to trust her, to want to protect her. But if Beckett protects her, then they will too. I have no doubt about that. They are no longer loyal to the Retribution Kings. They are loyal to Beckett. Any man who can earn the loyalty of others like that is worthy of marrying Rialta.

I'm focusing on Beckett's men when Vincent's words draw me back into his conversation.

"If you don't marry my daughter, then I'll kill Ri."

My heart stops.

I'm not afraid to die; I never have been. In fact, I'm surprised I've survived this long. And Vincent doesn't make a threat he's not willing to act on. If Beckett doesn't marry Rialta, then Vincent will kill me.

I wish I could shut my ears off because I don't want to hear Beckett's response. I don't want to hear if he cares about me. I don't want to hear he has any feelings for me.

His feelings will change. They will grow to love Rialta. She's incredible and worthy, and he will find a way to love her. He's fallen in love countless times. I have no doubt he will again.

Beckett is a romantic, though. He believes in his one true love. He's never said that, but it's why he's so disappointed and heartbroken when his relationships end. He always thinks she was the one for him. What he doesn't realize is there is no such thing as the one, no such thing as one great love. We can love many people. We can fall in love with our enemies or our friends. We can fall in love without meaning to, but that doesn't mean that person is worthy of our love.

No, he will fall in love with her in time. What is more worrying is whether or not she will fall in love with him. *Will she ever accept him?*

I fell in love with him easily, even when I shouldn't have. It's not my fault—not really. I had no memories of my role in Rialta's life, and Beckett is so damn easy to fall in love with.

I look down at Rialta standing at the end of the aisle, looking at Beckett carefully. She doesn't give any indication of how she feels. I was surprised when Vincent told her she was to get married tonight, and she didn't protest. She didn't cry, throw a tantrum, or demand to at least meet the man a handful of times first. She didn't do any of those things. She simply heard her instructions and agreed to them.

Vincent seemed pleased, but I had my suspicions. I still do. I haven't seen Rialta in years. She's grown and matured a lot in the time since I last saw her, but she's still young. Marrying a man you don't know, even a good man like Beckett, is still a big deal.

But Rialta did as she was told without a fuss, without even the slightest protest.

As I study Rialta now, I can see a hint of the truth. She's terrified. Her skin is pale, her eyes are dilated, and I'm pretty sure I can see a bead of sweat dripping down from her forehead through my rifle scope. She's going to be a problem as much as Beckett will be.

As Vincent finishes threatening Beckett, a fight doesn't break out, surprisingly. Beckett simply holds out his arm to Rialta, and she takes it. They turn to face the minister, and he continues with the ceremony.

I can't breathe. I don't know what to think.

I'm not going to be able to shut out this next part. I'm going to hear them speak every vow. I'm going to hear them speak every promise to each other. They will be with each other forever—until one of them dies.

Beckett will never be mine.

I will have to spend my life watching the two of them as a married couple.

Even though my heart is bursting with agony now, it will heal. There is no such thing as one great love anyway. I will find another man to love or lust after. Beckett wasn't special in that way, but he will be a good fit for Rialta.

"Do you, Rialta Corsi, take Beckett Monroe to be your husband?" the minister asks.

Please, ears, turn off.

I stare down at Rialta, waiting for her to say the magic words. It will kill me, but Beckett's 'I do' in response will end me.

The words never come—from either of them.

Instead, Rialta falls to the ground.

No!

I want to run to her, jump down from my hiding spot in the rafters and scoop her up in my arms. My instincts are yelling at me to do that, but my training tells me to wait. I shouldn't reveal myself. Vincent can help her as easily as I can. My job is to stay here and watch from the rafters until a more clear need presents itself.

If she was shot, I need to stay up here to return fire.

If she just fainted, then I'm not really needed, even if it's difficult to stay away.

Then Beckett does something that proves his value to Rialta more than anything else. He catches her head, preventing her from hitting the ground.

He whistles for his men to surround her, and he drapes his body over hers. If she is under attack, no more bullets will hit her. He leans in close, quickly checking her vitals, assessing what happened to her.

My breath eases. My pulse relaxes.

Vincent catches my attention and gives me a pleased nod.

I chose the right man for Rialta. Beckett will do everything he can to protect her; that's who he is. He's a good man. He's a man who falls in love a little too easily. Most importantly, he's a man who protects the innocent. He protects those who are worthy of protection.

Beckett has claimed time and time again that he isn't my hero. He was right—I never needed a hero.

But he sure as hell is hers.

3

BECKETT

WITH A QUICK WHISTLE, all of my men surround Rialta, ensuring no harm comes to her. I may not want to marry her, but she doesn't deserve to die. She's young, innocent, and most likely being as forced to marry me as I am her.

"Is she bleeding?" Hayes asks.

I feel over the back of her head and dress. "I don't see anything obvious."

"Other than Corsi's snipers in the ceiling, I don't see anyone that would be attacking us," Lennox says.

Gage pulls up his phone and types furiously. "There aren't any security cameras in the church, and I don't see anyone from the cafe across the street."

I nod. "If we were under attack, the snipers would be shooting like crazy right now. I think she just fainted."

"I don't blame the poor girl after she took one look at you," Hayes teases.

"Jokes right now, Hayes?" Lennox barks.

I ignore them both as I place my hand on Rialta's neck to check her pulse. My eyes cut to Vincent, who is still seated in the first pew, watching us closely. He doesn't run to his daughter's side. He obviously doesn't feel like whatever happened is very serious. That or he trusts me—like really, really trusts me. He trusts me with his daughter's life. I suck in a breath at that thought.

That's what the games were about. He wanted to figure out who among us could be trusted with his daughter, not just who would be the best leader. In fact, it wouldn't shock me if the main reason I won is that they think I'm the best at keeping her safe.

Ri has called me a hero numerous times. It hits me now that she wasn't looking for a hero for herself, but for this woman, whoever she is, and whatever relation she has to Ri.

I frown as I continue to feel her pulse.

"What's wrong?" Hayes asks.

"Her pulse is extremely weak, and her breaths are too shallow. We need to get her to a hospital ASAP," I snap.

Hayes's eyes widen, and Lennox helps me scoop Rialta up in my arm.

Vincent is finally on his feet as he realizes this isn't about a scared girl fainting. This is some sort of medical emergency.

"I'll call an ambulance," Vincent says.

"No, it will be faster if we drive. We have a first aid kit in the car," I say.

Vincent pockets his phone. "My men and I will follow you. Don't let her die." He eyes me, and the threat is obvious. If she dies, so do I.

I nod and run behind Lennox and Hayes as I carry Rialta against me. Gage takes up the rear with Corsi behind him.

I see men starting to drop from the rafters and running after us. For a second, I want to stay and see if Ri is among them. I'm still not entirely convinced she's alive. I still think this could be a switch. Ri died, and Corsi found a lookalike to take her place, not accepting that he doesn't have an heir.

But this woman in my arms, whoever she is, deserves to live. I'll have to find Ri later.

We race to our SUV parked outside the church. Lennox is already in the driver's seat. Hayes has the first aid kit out and the back door open. I climb inside with Rialta in my arm while Gage hops into the front seat.

The second we are all in, Lennox steps on the gas.

Hayes reaches across and tests her pulse. "She still has a pulse; it's just really weak."

I nod. I can't really assess her with most of her body resting against my arm, but I feel her chest rising slowly against me.

"What do you think is wrong with her? Did she just faint?" Hayes asks.

I look down at the woman. She's skinny, far too skinny, now that I have a better look at her. Her skin is still pale, almost yellow, and I can't find muscle anywhere on her body.

"I don't think this is just about fainting. I think this is something else," I say ominously.

All eyes in the car land on me, but no one says anything. Less than five minutes later, Lennox pulls the car in front of an emergency room. Gage has my door open before I can even move for it, and he helps me get Rialta out of the car.

We are met at the door by medical staff pushing a

gurney. I gently place Rialta on the bed and run by her side as they roll her through the hospital doors. The others are right on our tail as we enter the hospital. Their guns would be drawn if it wouldn't draw too much suspicion.

They push her into a private room, and a nurse turns to us immediately. "Everyone who isn't family, get out," she says.

Lennox, Hayes, and Gage all look to me, waiting for me to tell them what to do.

I nod. They can protect her just as well outside the room as they can inside it. And the nurses and doctors need room to work.

They leave the room, and the nurse turns to me.

"I'm family," I say, keeping it simple.

She examines me in my suit and then looks at her wedding dress, piecing things together. She pats me on the shoulder and then turns to begin helping them work on Rialta.

I slink into the corner. I'm guessing whether they believe I'm family or not, it's just a matter of time before I'm kicked out too if things turn south.

I watch as an IV is placed, her dress is cut from her body, pads are placed on her chest and hooked up to wires, and an oxygen mask is placed over her face. There is no obvious sign of what's wrong with her. I can see her chest still rising and falling, and her heart rate is starting to show up on the monitor, so she's still alive.

I should want her dead. That's the easiest way to get out of having to marry her, but I can't wish death on someone so innocent. And whatever it means for me, I won't allow her to die.

A second later, Corsi appears in the doorway of her

room. He quickly walks to the side of her bed and takes her hand in his, moisture pooling in his eyes.

He tries to speak to her, but the second he opens his mouth, tears start streaming down his face. He gets choked up and can't get the words out. He's still gripping her hand as her heart starts to flatline.

A nurse pushes him back into the corner opposite me as they go to work on restarting her heart. The paddles come out, and they shock her heart.

Corsi nearly collapses in the corner at the sight. I've never seen him so broken, so vulnerable. He's supposed to be this fearless, ruthless leader, not a stumbling man consumed by his emotions.

I turn my attention back to the screen, but it's still flatlining. My eyes widen as I look at the beautiful woman, so young and on the brink of death. It's not fair. I don't know who she is, but she doesn't deserve this.

A nurse performs CPR while they wait to try again to shock her heart. It can't be more than a couple of seconds before the paddles come down on her chest again, but it feels like a lifetime to me. I can't imagine what it feels like to Corsi.

And then—life.

The line goes up and down on the machine, and if I look closely at Rialta, I can see her chest rise and fall.

An uneasy relief washes through everyone in the room. She survived this time, but there is no guarantee she'll endure the next incident.

One of the nurses looks to Corsi, then me. "We need to clear the room, so we have more space to work."

Corsi's eyes widen, and he opens his mouth to protest, but his throat runs dry. No words come out of the most feared leader in Chicago.

The nurse is right—Corsi shouldn't stay here. Whatever happens, he shouldn't see any more.

I walk over to Corsi. "Go. I won't leave her side no matter what happens; you have my word."

Corsi's eyes narrow at me; he'll hold me to my promise. But it's a promise I'd make whether I want to get in Corsi's good graces or not.

Rialta doesn't deserve to be alone right now.

I push Corsi toward the door as I take Rialta's hand.

The nurse who ordered us to leave gives me a look.

"I'm not leaving. You can call security, but they'll be knocked out on the floor before they even enter the room. You've seen the guys outside. You know who I work for. I'm not leaving," I threaten.

The nurse frowns but doesn't argue anymore. I remain by Rialta's side, holding her hand while the doctors and nurses work. I'm not sure Rialta is going to make it until twenty minutes later, when I feel her squeeze my hand back. It's then that I know she's still in there. I realize Rialta and Ri do have something in common—they're both fighters.

An hour later, Rialta is finally stable enough to be moved to a recovery room. We're left alone after they've settled her.

She hasn't woken up fully yet, and I haven't let go of her hand.

I can't help but wonder what's wrong with her. Normal twenty-something young women don't faint like that. Their hearts don't just stop like that. They don't have to get rushed to the hospital like that.

I hope I can have a moment alone with her to ask. Although I'm sure Gage has already pulled up all her medical files and has all the answers.

There's a soft knock on the door, though. My time alone with Rialta is about to be up. I assume it's Corsi or one of the nurses coming back to check on her. But familiar chills race up my spine, telling me it's not Corsi standing at the foot of Rialta's bed.

I turn and see Ri—she's alive.

4

RI

BECKETT IS HOLDING Rialta's hand as she lies unconscious in her hospital bed. He's already so good at protecting and taking care of her. I know I chose the right man for the job.

I thought it would hurt seeing him take care of her. But right now, all I care about is that she's alive, and he's holding her hand when I can't.

"Is she okay?" I ask, my voice unusually soft and timid.

Beckett blinks, not believing his eyes that I'm here.

I take a step closer and can see Rialta take deep, slow breaths in her sleep. She's going to make it.

"You're alive," Beckett says in shock.

"Yes, why wouldn't I be?" I ask.

He shakes his head, and I can see tears welling in his eyes. "When I lifted that veil and saw it wasn't you, I was so terrified you were dead. I thought Corsi found a lookalike to replace you as quickly as possible before word of your death spread."

I swallow the lump in my throat. "Well, as you can see, I'm very much alive."

The air between us changes, supercharging with tension.

I should leave.

I don't even know why I came. I just needed to see Rialta is fine with my own eyes and—

In the next second, Beckett has his arm around me, pulling my head tight against his chest and holding me so tight I'm afraid he'll never let go.

"Lennox!" Beckett hollers out into the hallway.

Lennox appears at the door, staring at me like he's seen a ghost.

I sigh.

"Hold Rialta's hand and watch over her until I get back," Beckett orders him.

He nods and takes Beckett's place by Rialta's bedside.

I raise an eyebrow.

Beckett doesn't say more as he takes my hand and drags me out of the hospital room. He doesn't stop to let me talk to Gage or Hayes, who guard the door and give me questioning looks as we walk by. Beckett is on a mission to get me alone, and I don't resist. Maybe I should, but I don't.

He continues to yank my hand, leading me out of the hospital. Once outside, he doesn't stop until we've reached an empty alleyway around the corner. With a tug of his hand, he spins me to face him. We are all but touching, staring each other down.

"Start talking," he orders.

I furrow my brow, annoyed with his tone.

"You're not pregnant?" he asks.

I shake my head. "No, I'm not."

"You're not hurt?"

"No."

His eyes roam my body, looking for any evidence of injuries. Once he's satisfied, he makes his move.

I don't anticipate it, so I'm taken off guard when his lips crash down on mine. I should push him away, but I'm so desperate for the kiss that I literally can't. Not only do I let him, but I kiss him back.

Our bodies slam together, and my hands lock around the back of his head as I deepen the kiss. I love everything about kissing him. I love how his tongue tastes, how his lips feel, and the deep throaty growls that vibrate through his neck. My panties soak with every swipe of his tongue against mine under the moonlight.

In the dark, our kisses are hidden. But once dawn arrives, there will be no hiding.

I put my hand on his chest and gently push him away. I can't keep letting myself fall for this man. I can't keep letting my emotions get in the way.

Beckett grasps my hand in his, but he doesn't fight me. He doesn't try to kiss me again.

He looks deep into my eyes, searching for the truth I've kept hidden from him. It's a truth I've hidden for a long time.

"My job is to protect Rialta Corsi. It's been my job practically my entire life," I say.

Beckett's eyes dart side to side as he looks into mine. His eyes alone ask a million questions.

I'll answer some of them, but probably not enough to fully satisfy him.

"Vincent decided early on that the best way to protect her was to hide her away, while I agreed to pretend to be her."

Beckett frowns but doesn't interrupt or ask any questions.

"I went along with being hypnotized by Kek so I would truly believe I was her, to keep her hidden. I only recently remembered the truth when Kek reversed the hypnotization."

Beckett takes in my words, only revealing the most basic outline.

"What's wrong with Rialta?" he asks.

"Nothing."

He narrows his eyes. "Why would you agree to living a fake life? Why risk your life to protect her? Why find a husband for her?"

"She's worth protecting."

"What about you? Is your life not worth protecting?"

"I can take care of myself." I rip my hand from his grasp.

"I know that, but it doesn't mean you should take extra risks for someone else."

"It was worth it," I protest.

"So everything between us, it was all a lie? You never felt anything for me? Were you just trying to find a good husband for Rialta? Someone who could take up your mantel and protect her?"

"Yes," I breathe.

That single word is more of a lie than anything I've ever said or done before. I do love Beckett. And I love Rialta, that's why they're perfect for each other.

His head drops in disbelief.

"What's your name? Ri? Something else?"

I open my mouth but hesitate. It's been so long since I've used my own name since anyone actually said my name aloud. I lick my lips and speak.

"My name is River."

"River," Beckett tests my name on his lips, and my heart explodes.

"River what?"

I shrug. "I was adopted. I never knew my last name, but I guess it's Corsi now."

"River Corsi," he says hesitantly, still getting used to the way it sounds, just as I am.

"You can keep calling me Ri, though," I say.

He bites his bottom lip, considering it—likely considering a lot of things.

He circles around me as he thinks.

I close my eyes as I feel his gaze on me, trying not to let him see how he affects me. How my body heats with his gaze on me. How my skin crawls, itching for him to touch me again, to kiss me.

That was the last time I'll ever kiss him, and it wasn't enough. It's never enough. I could kiss him a million times, and it wouldn't be enough.

Fuck.

"Open your eyes," he says.

I do, hoping I'm not giving away any feelings.

He once again searches my eyes, but if he sees anything, he doesn't tell me.

"So what now?" he asks.

I clear my throat. "You marry Rialta Corsi. I continue to protect her as one of her guards, and you slowly fall in love with her. In the meantime, Vincent will teach you how he runs things and prepare you to take over for him. I assume the Retribution Kings have already disowned you. Luckily Vincent's empire is bigger than the Retribution Kings's, so you'll have plenty of power over them."

"You think I'm after power?" His eyebrows shoot up, and he scowls.

"No," I say.

"Then why would I marry Rialta? What do I get out of it?"

"You believe in one true love, don't you?"

"Yes," he says.

"She's it. I've spent weeks getting to know you. I know you better than anyone. And I know her better than anyone. She's your match in every way. She needs a hero—and whether you want to admit it or not, you play the hero role well, Beckett."

His face darkens. "I don't believe I'll ever fall in love again—not after all my failed attempts."

I wince, knowing he's including me.

"I don't want love. I don't want power," he says.

"What do you want?"

His heated stare is his only response. My throat tightens, my skin warms, and my pulse races through me. *Please stop wanting me. It would be so much easier.*

"I won't marry Rialta."

"You won the game. That was the rule. You win; you marry her. Then, once you produce an heir, you take over Vincent's role as leader of the mafia."

"Well, you should offer the position to the runner-up because I don't want it."

I frown, glaring at him.

"You'll marry her," I say.

"I won't."

"You'll marry Rialta, or I die."

He frowns. "Corsi wouldn't kill you. You've been too invaluable to him for far too long. He would be killing his daughter's protector—one of his most valuable assets. I don't believe he'll actually kill you."

"You're willing to take that risk?" I ask.

He sucks in a hiss; he'll do anything to keep me alive. His feelings for me haven't changed yet. But soon enough, Rialta will be his whole world. He'll do everything he can for her, and I'll be nothing but a distant memory.

"Trust me when I say that Vincent will do anything to protect Rialta—anything. That includes killing me, so think twice before you refuse to marry her," I beg.

5

BECKETT

RIVER—THAT'S her name. Not Ri, not Rialta, not Princess, not Fighter—River.

River Corsi.

I always knew she was a Corsi, but I didn't realize how deep the bonds run. I'm still not sure I fully understand. It's not about blood—there's some other reason she stays and works for that man and his family.

Ri—River—will die if I don't marry Rialta. That's what she says. That's what Corsi said.

I don't want to believe either of them, but I do. Corsi is a brutal, ruthless man. The lengths he's taken to protect his daughter make it clear how much he loves her. He's willing to do anything for Rialta.

River and he have the same goal—to protect Rialta at all costs. They think I'm the man who can keep her safe. I don't understand why, but they will stop at nothing to ensure our marriage happens.

I know what I have to do.

I return to the hospital on my own; River doesn't

follow me. Although, I'm sure River at least plans to hide in the shadows with a sniper rifle on me in case I don't follow through.

I head back to Rialta's room. All three of the guys are standing outside when I approach.

"I thought I told you to stay with Rialta until I got back," I snap at Lennox.

"Corsi is in there with her. I didn't think it was appropriate for me to stay," Lennox answers.

I nod and then rap my knuckles against the door before entering.

Rialta is still asleep in her bed, with Corsi sitting in the chair next to her bed. He looks up at me with tears still in his eyes. He doesn't wipe them away or try to hide in shame at showing his weakness so clearly to me. His greatest weakness is his daughter.

I stand at the foot of her bed, unsure if this is the appropriate place to have this conversation or not.

Corsi stands to lead me out of the room but stops a few feet away from me, facing me.

"River chose well. I wasn't sure, but I trusted her. She has a sixth sense when it comes to things like this. You and Rialta will make a good match," Corsi says.

"Why? Why not trust Rialta to find her own husband?" I pause. "Actually, why does Rialta need a husband at all? She seems plenty strong enough. And if she isn't, then River and your men seem more than capable of protecting her."

"I don't have to explain myself to you," he snaps.

"Maybe you should if you're willing to pass your daughter and everything you've built to me."

Corsi frowns but doesn't open his mouth. He doesn't

speak. He doesn't offer me any explanation, and he probably never will. But it doesn't matter; that's not what I came here for.

"I'll marry Rialta under one condition."

"You aren't in a position to be making conditions."

I glare at him. "Actually, I am. You need a husband for your daughter. And your threat to kill Ri, while real enough, is something you'd really like to avoid. So I'll make this easier on both of us. There will be no more death threats or manipulation. We will work together in a partnership."

Corsi doesn't say anything, giving me his full attention. I don't understand why he wants his daughter married so badly, but I do know he doesn't want to spill any more blood. He just wants this game over, and Rialta married.

"I'll marry Rialta if you protect my brother and his family. Put a stop to the war between the gangs. Stop Odette. Then, I'll marry your daughter."

It's a lot to ask, I know. But if I'm going to marry Rialta, I might as well get something worthy out of it. I need my family to be safe.

I have three amazing guys who would die for me outside this room, but they alone aren't enough to stop the war. The Retribution Kings are no longer mine to control either. I need an army to stop this war and ensure my brother, Enzo, and his family are safe.

I won't marry Rialta for anything less.

Corsi looks me up and down. "River was right. You drive a hard bargain. But I can see how clearly you're a perfect fit for my daughter, so I'll do you this favor."

I let out an exhale of relief.

"But…I can't stop the war. I won't send my men to their deaths."

I frown. "If you don't, our deal is off."

"I can't stop the war, but I can ensure that Enzo Black and his family are safe. Is that good enough for you, Beckett?" Corsi says.

I consider his words, making sure I'm not missing anything. Corsi is careful with his words, and he'll hold me to the deal whether it's a good deal for me or not.

It would be better if he stopped the war, not just ensured my family is safe, but I doubt I'll get a better offer from him.

I don't know what will happen after I marry Rialta. I don't know if I'll grow to care for her. I don't know if I'll ever get over Ri. I don't know what Corsi will require of me to take over his position—not that I want it.

But I'll do anything to protect Ri and my family. This deal will ensure that Ri isn't harmed and that my brother and his family are safe.

I hold out my hand to Corsi.

He takes it, and we shake.

"I'll ensure your family is safe," Corsi says.

"After my family is safe, I'll marry your daughter."

As we shake, I feel eyes on us. I turn and see Rialta sitting up in bed, wide awake.

I lock eyes with her for the first time since she passed out in the church. She looks at me suspiciously, and I don't blame her. I gaze back at her in equal measure, unsure of what our future holds. There's a very good chance that we are going to end up as husband and wife, whether either of us wants it or not.

She doesn't know if I'm a good man, and I don't know the kind of woman she is. Yet, I don't see fear in her eyes. I see determination.

If she learned that look from Ri, then I should be terrified. That look can only mean she's as strong-willed as Ri, and I know I'm no match against the two of them.

6
RI

I PULL into the driveway of a countryside house while Rialta sleeps in the backseat. Beckett sits next to her, staring out the window. His eyes never made contact with mine in the rearview mirror as we drove, but that could be because I rarely look in the rearview mirror.

I don't know what changed Beckett's mind. *Was it our conversation? Or did he have a different talk with Corsi?*

I park the car in the driveway. Rialta is still asleep.

"I'll go secure the house before you two come in," I say, getting out of the car and not waiting for Beckett to reply.

I'm relieved to be out of the car. It felt stifling in there, trapped with the two of them. It's going to be worse trapped in this house with them, though. I'll be trapped forever as I watch them get married and share their lives together.

If I'm lucky, they'll fire me, and I won't have to suffer much longer.

I head into the house with my gun drawn, ready for anything. The house is small—only two bedrooms, one bathroom, an eat-in kitchen, and a small living room with a fireplace. But it's in the middle of nowhere and safe—that's all that matters.

I take my time going clearing the house. It gives me more time before I have to see Rialta or Beckett. We're here for her to heal and for them to get to know each other before they get married.

This trip is also giving Vincent time to fulfill whatever end of a deal he struck with Beckett to get him to agree so easily. There has to be a deal; that has to be the reason that Beckett is here without a fight. That or Beckett is just buying time to find an out.

After I've checked every room twice, I finally head back out to the car. They're right where I left them—Beckett looking out the window deep in thought and Rialta asleep next to him.

"All clear," I say as I open Rialta's door and gently wake her.

She opens her eyes, and Beckett finally looks in my direction.

I ignore him and give Rialta all my attention. That's my strategy for surviving this hell.

"How are you feeling?" I ask her.

She yawns. "Just sleepy."

"Well, let's get you into the house and into bed. Then you can sleep until you can't sleep anymore," I say.

Rialta smiles at me. "I've missed you."

"I've missed you too," I say.

I offer her my hand to help her out of the car. She takes it easily and seems steady on her feet. I barely have to help her.

I hear a door slam behind us and assume Beckett is right behind us. I turn my head to look when I feel Rialta's grasp slipping.

I try to catch her to keep her on her feet, but Beckett beats me to it. He catches her in his arm.

"Dizzy?" he asks her in his deep, inviting voice.

She nods.

"I can carry you if you want?"

"That's probably for the best if we don't want to have to immediately turn around and head back to the nearest hospital," she says.

He nods solemnly. Then he effortlessly scoops her up in his arm and carries her up the three steps to the front porch of the house.

I run ahead and hold the front door open as he carries her into the house. I can't help but notice how intensely Rialta looks at Beckett. I can't help but notice that he doesn't seem annoyed by her stare.

Jesus, I'm reading way too much into a look. He's just being nice and carrying her into the house.

"Which room?" Beckett asks me.

"The primary is on the right," I answer.

I take my time following after them, although I don't wait long enough. Just as I walk into the room, Beckett tucks her into bed and kisses her forehead. He sits down on the edge of her bed, clearly with no intention of leaving.

"I'll just leave you two alone. Holler if you need anything, Rialta."

"Wait," Rialta says.

I stop. "Need something? Food? Water?"

"Actually..." Rialta looks from Beckett to me. "I need to talk to River by myself."

"I'll start working on dinner," Beckett says, standing and walking toward me, toward the door.

The room is barely big enough for the queen-sized

bed and dresser. When Beckett gets to me, there is nowhere for me to move out of the way.

He looks at me as he brushes past me, seemingly holding words back. Our shoulders nudge each other, and our fingers graze ever so slightly, sending a tingling of electricity through my body.

I ignore the feeling and walk to the side of Rialta's bed as Beckett closes the door on his way out.

I force a smile. "I'm so happy you're back. We have so much to catch up on."

"We do, but since our father thinks I need to get married immediately, we should focus on that," she replies.

I nod. "You're probably right." Although, her marriage to Beckett is the last thing I want to think about.

Her head falls back against the bed frame, and she yawns again. She's still exhausted from yesterday. She needs to sleep for a couple of days, and then she'll feel a lot better.

"Tell me about Beckett. Tell me what he's like. Tell me why you chose him for me," she says.

Oh, fuck me.

I don't want to have this conversation even though I love her to death. She's my best friend, the person I would die for, but this will be complete torture.

"Beckett is stubborn. He thinks he's right and everyone else is wrong. He won't let you win an argument with him. He doesn't express his feelings easily. In fact, you have to work really hard to get him to open up at all. He's loyal to a fault. He likes being in control and is bossy as hell," I start.

"You're not really making a case for why I should want to marry him."

"I'm just telling you all the facts. You need to know the

good parts and the bad. But I was just getting to the good part." I smile. "Beckett is the best friend you'll ever have. He would take a bullet for you."

"Don't you mean he'd take a bullet for his friends?"

"No, he'd take a bullet for you because he knows you're innocent. He'd take a bullet for anyone he considers innocent. He protects his family and those he loves even harder. He's funny, sweet, and a great kisser." I wiggle my eyebrows, and she laughs.

I consider telling her he's an even greater lover, but I don't know how much she knows. And admitting you've fucked someone's future husband probably isn't a great way to restart our friendship.

"Beckett's good-looking," Rialta says in a dreamy voice.

"That he is," I agree, but try not to think too hard about his rippling muscles and sexy smirk. I clear my throat.

"He lost one of his arms a few years back in an explosion, and that makes others look down on him like he's weak. But he's not weak—in fact, he's the opposite. He's a better fighter than almost any man I've ever met."

"A better fighter than you?" she asks.

"Well, no one's better than me."

She laughs. "You haven't changed much."

"Neither have you." I sit on the bed and pull her against my body like she's my little sister. I guess, in many ways, she is.

"What else?" she asks.

"He's not looking for power like most of the men we know. He's a good leader when he has to be, but he'd prefer to live a life without all the power."

"Good. I'd hate for him to be too much like Father."

"He's nothing like Vincent. Beckett is kind. He's gentle. He'll treat you like a princess," I say.

He'll probably call her that too. My heart takes a stabbing as I think about him using the same nicknames on her as he did me. "He'll pamper you, take you on romantic dates, and be a great husband."

Her face sobers. "How do you know? What if he hates me?"

I grab her chin and turn it gently to face me. "You, Rialta Corsi, are a great catch. In fact, dozens of men fought to their deaths to date you."

"They fought to the death for you," she says.

"No, they didn't. They fought for you. They didn't know who I was. As soon as they learned I know how to use a gun, they hated the idea of me. You were born for your role. You are meant to be a princess, Rialta. Beckett is your prince. He's a great hero."

"Maybe."

Beckett is going to have to do some of the convincing himself, but I have one last thing to add.

"Beckett is a romantic. He's been searching all his life for his one true love. He's failed, married the wrong person even. But he still wants it. All you have to do is let him in. Let him see how amazing, sweet, and caring you are. Let him see how big your heart is.

"Show him how you'll make an excellent mafia queen by his side. You'll be an incredible mother to his children. Let him see the real you, and I have no doubt he'll fall in love with you. And this time when he falls, it will be with the right woman."

A knock at the door makes us both jump, cutting off Rialta's response to my speech.

"Come in," Rialta says once she regains her composure.

Beckett opens the door and holds out a bottle of pills and water. "It's time for you to take your medications."

Rialta smiles at him brightly. "Thank you."

He walks in and over to her side of the bed. He helps her open the bottle and take her pills.

But his eyes are on me. He heard at least the last part of what I said, and he's not happy about it.

7

BECKETT

"Need anything else?" I ask Rialta as she yawns hard again. She's tired, and the meds make her even more tired, so she's not going to last much longer. Any conversation the two of us need to have will have to wait. Besides, she's not really the woman I want to talk to anyway.

"I'm good," she says, smiling at me like I'm her angel.

Fuck. I'm not her angel. I'm not her hero. I'm not her anything.

I nod and leave the room, my blood boiling from what I overheard River say.

I'm barely out the door when I hear the bedroom door close and footsteps behind me.

I'm back in the kitchen, pulling out vegetables to chop when River walks in.

"Rialta's asleep," she says.

"She couldn't possibly fall asleep that fast."

She laughs. "Then you don't know Rialta very well. Even before all this, she could fall asleep at the snap of her fingers and in the most uncomfortable of places."

"That's just the thing—I don't know Rialta. Just like I don't know you," I snap.

She stills at my words but doesn't give a quick retort.

I carry carrots, celery, and onion over to a chopping board. I go to work on the onion first, chopping away hard and fast. It's harder to chop vegetables when you only have one hand.

I could lean forward and use my residual limb to hold the vegetable while I chop. I could put something next to the vegetable to keep it from moving. But I do neither. I chop wildly, letting the onion fly around the chopping board. The pieces I chop won't be pretty, but I don't give a damn about that right now.

"Stop trying to make her like me," I say, chopping down so hard that a piece of onion juice flies at my face. I welcome the sting in my eye, wiping it off with the back of my shirt before chopping some more.

River looks at me with concern, but she knows better than to say anything while I have a knife in my hand.

"Why? Isn't it better if she likes you?"

"No," I say.

She frowns defiantly, crossing her arms in front of her chest.

"You made a deal with Vincent. I know you did; it's the only reason you intend on marrying her. And if you plan on marrying her, then I'm going to do everything I can to make the marriage work. I'm going to help her like you. And if you weren't so stubborn, I'd help you fall for her too," she lectures at me.

I slam the knife down harder, making her jump.

"What was the deal you made, Beckett?"

Of course, that's all she cares about. "Corsi will keep my brother and his family safe."

"Good, they should be safe. I was worried about them," she confesses.

I stop chopping and slowly put the knife down, lifting my head to glare at her. "Don't feel sorry for them. Don't feel sorry for any of my family, River." I say her name like a curse. To me, she'll always be Ri, short for Rialta. I don't know who this River person is.

"I don't feel sorry for them. I just don't like that they got twisted up in this whole mess."

"A mess you started." I pick up the knife and point it in her direction.

She sighs. "I was just protecting my family, the same as you."

I shake my head and begin to hack at the celery, but it's not enough to avoid the daggers she's shooting my way with her eyes.

"What are you making, anyway?" she asks.

I don't lift my head to look at her. "Chicken noodle soup. I thought it would help Rialta feel better."

She doesn't respond, but I feel a shift in her gaze. I don't want to look at her, but eventually, I can't resist. When I look up, I see admiration and love in her eyes.

"You're such a romantic, Hero."

"I'm not a romantic or a hero. Besides, I love chicken noodle soup. This is as much for me as it is for her."

"Uh-huh."

Great, now she thinks I'm already halfway in love with Rialta just because I'm making her this damn soup.

"Need any help?"

"No," I snap.

She sighs but doesn't say anything else. I keep chopping furiously, trying to remember how I got here and trying to find a way out of this situation.

The first step is to wait for word that Enzo and his family are safe. Until I get verification from Lennox and the others, I won't trust anything Corsi says. I need them safe; then I can figure out my predicament here.

I'm deep in thought when I feel pain rip through my index finger.

"Fucking hell," I curse as blood spills down my hand onto my wrist.

River is by my side before I even realize what happened. She grabs several paper towels and bunches them around my finger, applying pressure.

"The first aid kit is in the bathroom. Although, I should put a first aid kit in every room of this house. You two are the clumsiest people I know," she groans.

I frown. "You know I could lose my finger while you're making jokes."

"Drama queen. You're not going to lose your finger." She yanks on my hand, and I have no choice but to follow her to the bathroom.

The tiny, desperately needing renovation bathroom.

There's a small tub but no shower head. The toilet is smashed up right against the edge of the tub. The single sink looks like it hasn't been used in years, sitting atop a cabinet falling off its hinges. The rest of the house is mostly functional, except for this room.

"I know, I wish the bathroom was better, but this is the best I could find to rent without drawing suspicion," River says, applying pressure with one hand to my wound. She opens the cabinet door, sticking her hand inside to search for the supposed first aid kit.

"Found it!" Thankfully the first aid kit looks a whole lot newer than this bathroom. River sets the first aid kit on the sink before opening it. She quickly takes stock of the supplies before turning her attention back to my finger.

"Alright, let's see how bad it is."

She unwraps the paper towels now saturated with my blood. She cocks her head to the side as she examines my index finger.

"It's pretty deep. It could use stitches, but there aren't any in this first aid kit. I think I have some in the car—"

"Just bandage it. I'll be fine," I quip.

She raises an eyebrow as she yanks my arm under the sink and turns on the water to rinse the wound.

I wince as water pours over my cut.

She turns the faucet off and grabs an alcohol swab. "Don't scream in pain. Rialta is a deep sleeper, but she's not that deep of a sleeper."

"I won't scream," I sigh.

She rubs the alcohol on the wound, and I shift uncomfortably, wincing and biting my bottom lip to keep from making a sound.

When she stops, it's with a knowing grin. "Stings, doesn't it?"

"Nope," I lie. It burned like hell, worse than the initial injury.

She simply shakes her head. She pulls bandages out of the first aid kit and wraps them around my finger until the blood is no longer leaking down my hand. Then she finds a washcloth under the sink, wets it, and wipes the dried blood from my hand and arm.

"I still can't figure out how you cut yourself," she says.

I shrug, not really sure either. My hand must have slipped forward as the blade was coming down.

"You know you should really be more careful. You only have five fingers—none to spare. And you were always better at making me come with your fingers instead of your tongue. I wouldn't want you to lose your best feature," she teases.

"Seems like you'll be missing out either way unless Rialta is into an open relationship."

River's face drops as if, for a split second, she forgot. She forgot about Rialta. She forgot that we can never be together again if I marry her. She forgot everything and just let her guard down with me.

River clears her throat. "Well, you know how I feel about group sex, but I'm pretty sure Rialta doesn't like to share. You don't like sharing either. It's another reason why you two are perfect for each other."

I don't say anything. I try to look past her words. I try to understand the game she's playing.

She said she never had feelings for me. Everything between us was just a job. Her affections were all lies. She was just finding the best man for the job.

And yet...

I know the truth. She can't hide it from me any more than I can hide my feelings from her. Ri may be River, and I may have a monstrous past, but it doesn't stop how we feel about each other.

In another life, we'd be together. We wouldn't have lied, fucked up, or hurt each other. We would have just loved each other. Our love would be simple and pure.

It's clear in the way River looks at me that she still has feelings for me. And it's clear in the way my heart speeds in response to that look that I still love her. I may also want to rip River's throat out for lying to me, for hurting me, for pretending she doesn't love me, but then I'd desperately want to put all the pieces of her back together.

I want to yell at her to stop protecting others and, for

once, just do what she wants. If she wants me, we'll fight every army in the world for our love.

But I know she can't stop protecting. It's one of the reasons I love her, and it's why she loves me. We protect those we love. We protect those who deserve our protection. We protect. We're both heroes, both protectors.

She's a bodyguard for her adopted sister.

I've always played the guard for my brother and his family.

I don't see a future without River in it. Rialta is great, and I'm sure I could learn to enjoy her company, but she's not River. She's been hiding away while River's been fighting to keep her alive.

There is only one River, and I want to give her the world. I just have to find a way for us to keep all the people we love safe before we can admit our love out loud again.

8

BECKETT

RIALTA SLEEPS THROUGH DINNER, and River and I keep our distance from one another after the incident in the bathroom. River's been on her phone, constantly monitoring the security system and cracking Rialta's door occasionally to check on her. She's been asleep every time.

I leave River in the living room while I slowly clean the kitchen with my bandaged hand. River found me some pain pills to pop if I want, but honestly, the ache in my finger is nothing. But I'm starting to run out of things to clean in the kitchen, which means I might have to interact with River.

I walk into the living room to see my worries are unfounded. River's snoring softly on the couch.

I smile down at her. When she's asleep, she can't argue with me. I like the arguing, but being able to look at her honestly is nice. Right now, I can look at her like I love her, and no one is here to stop me.

Her neck is craned on a pillow, and her feet are hanging over the edge of the small couch that isn't really large enough to sleep on.

This two-bedroom house is limited on sleeping arrangements. River fits better than I would on the only couch, but I'm not going to let her wake up with a backache and a crick in her neck.

I decide to risk waking her and carrying her to the second bedroom. I'm not sure how much I'm going to sleep tonight anyway.

I try to be gentle as I lift River, but it's a little difficult with only one arm and a bandaged finger. She doesn't stir when I lift her; she must be exhausted.

I carry her into the other bedroom only to find the couch may have been better. I have to turn sideways to carry her around the tiny bed that barely fits in the small room.

As I lower her to the bed, River stirs. She blinks as I pull back the covers under her legs and try to cover her with them.

"What are you doing?" she snaps.

"Putting you to bed."

"You can't do that. I have to stay awake. I have to make sure Rialta is safe. I have to—"

"What's your plan? Never sleep? It's after one in the morning. You're not going to do a very good job protecting her if you don't get some sleep," I say.

"But I haven't set the alarm system yet. I haven't—"

"You need to sleep. I'll make sure Rialta is safe."

"But—"

"Stop. You chose me because you thought I would make a good husband for Rialta. You chose me because you thought I could keep Rialta safe. So trust me."

She frowns, debating further argument in her head, but her escaping yawn forces her eyes to grow heavy again.

"What about you? Don't you need sleep?"

"I'll sleep after you've gotten some sleep," I reply.

She can't keep her eyes open any longer, and they drift all the way closed. A moment later, she's snoring softly again.

I shake my head. "Always have to argue."

I pull the covers up over her and kiss her forehead. I want to kiss so much more, but I won't push my luck.

I tiptoe out of the room and close the door carefully behind me when I hear Rialta say, "River?"

"It's Beckett," I say softly back, turning and cracking Rialta's door open.

"Come in."

I walk into the room. "How are you feeling? Are you hungry?"

Her stomach growls before she can respond, and she giggles. "Yep, I should eat."

"I have chicken noodle soup. Is that okay?"

She nods.

"Do you want to eat in here or the living room?"

She stretches her arms over her head, causing her shirt to ride up and reveal her flat stomach. I look away, not wanting to see any part of her naked body.

"Living room, I think. I don't think I'll fall back asleep for a little while, and there's no TV in here."

I walk over to her side. "Is it okay if I carry you again? I don't think you should try to walk until you've had some food and liquids in your system. I don't want you to get dizzy and faint again."

"That's probably for the best," she agrees.

I scoop her up and carry her to the living room couch River was just on. It feels different carrying the two women. Carrying River is about doing something nice for her. She is more than capable of walking herself, but I want to do it anyway as an act of love. Carrying Rialta is about necessity. She feels fragile, weak, and young.

I should ask for River's real age because she seems decades older than Rialta. The gap is not in terms of looks or beauty, but rather wisdom and experience. Rialta feels like a young woman, still figuring out who she is. River knows exactly who she is.

I help Rialta onto the couch before heading to the kitchen to warm up the soup. I return a few minutes later and sit down on the couch next to her, holding the bowl out to her.

"I couldn't find a tray. Do you want me to hold it, or can you hold the bowl yourself?"

Rialta reaches out to grab the bowl, but her hands are shaking.

"No worries, I can help you," I say.

She smiles tightly. I'm not sure if she likes being helped or not. I set the bowl on my lap and lift a spoonful of the soup up to her lips.

She leans forward and takes a small sip. "Oh my god, that's delicious. I was expecting that stuff you get out of the can, but this is homemade. Did you make it?"

I nod. I don't tell her it almost cost me a finger.

Her eyes twinkle as she looks at me.

"I'm not that good of a cook, so I wouldn't get used to it."

She laughs. "Don't worry; I won't get used to anything when it comes to you."

"What do you mean?"

She shrugs. "My life is not my own, not really. I've never made any decision for myself. I've never been given a choice in how I'm to live my life. Whether we marry or not, the decision isn't mine. And even if we get married, men don't survive long in our world. I can't count on anything."

I frown. "You can count on me, no matter what happens. You can count on me always being there for you."

Her eyes water. "Thank you, Beckett." She puts her hand on mine. Her hand is warm and clammy, nothing like River's. But I can tell she feels something when she touches me. "You really are a good guy, aren't you?"

I clear my throat. "I'm not sure I would say that."

She lowers her lips, and I lift another spoonful to her mouth. She bats her eyelashes down at me while eating the spoonful. "I would," she says.

I help her eat the rest of the bowl of soup. We don't speak, but she keeps flashing me looks that make me uncomfortable. Her flirty looks tell me she'd have no problem marrying me.

I set the bowl down on the end table. "You want to go back to bed?"

"No, I'm not really tired."

I nod. "How about a movie?"

Her face lights up at that. "Okay, what movie?"

I pick up one of the remotes. I flick the TV on but realize we don't have an internet or cable connection. There's a stack of DVDs in the corner, though.

I pick up a couple of boxes. "Are you a rom-com girl or an action girl?"

"Whatever you want."

"No, you choose," I say insistently. I don't know what this woman's life was in hiding. I don't know why she feels she has so little choice in her life, but I can at least let her pick the movie.

I hold up two DVDs I'm pretty sure she'll like based on what limited information I have on her. There's a stack of about fifty behind me, but we'd spend the whole night picking a movie if she had that many choices.

She scrunches her nose, looking between the two. "The one with the woman in the wedding dress."

I grin, knowing she'd pick that one. I pop the DVD in and sit next to her on the tiny couch that leaves no room for me to not touch her.

Our shoulders graze each other, and our hips touch as the movie starts.

I have so many questions to ask her, so many things I want to know. Mostly about River, but I don't ask any of them. I'll have time to ask questions—at least, I hope I will.

Right now, it's just about Rialta recovering and us getting to know each other. There will be time for us to talk.

The movie starts, but not five minutes later, Rialta's eyes start drifting closed. She won't last long out here.

I don't say anything as her eyes close, and her heavy head falls to my shoulder. Her breathing is slow and deep; she's already asleep. I'll move her soon back to her room, but I let her stay for now. It gives me a minute to look at her without her staring back.

She's a beautiful woman, just like River. Her long dark hair cascades down her neck, her lips are a stark contrast against her pale skin, and her eyes are full of life, even though her life has been a hard one.

I don't know what her wants and dreams are. I know she's not used to making choices for herself, but I suspect she still has dreams. She's hidden them well, possibly even from herself.

She doesn't have a choice in her life. Neither do I. Neither does River. But I vow then to find a way to give us all a choice in our futures. It's the only way any of us will be happy.

My phone buzzes in my pocket. I carefully shift so as not to wake Rialta as I pull my phone out. It's a text from Lennox.

Lennox: Corsi hasn't found your brother yet, but there is no sign that Odette or the Retribution Kings have found them either. I'll let you know when I have more to report.

Me: Thanks. Keep me updated.

I put my phone back with a sigh. I want to know Enzo and his family are safe. I want to know they have the protection of Corsi and the entire mafia.

But I also know that as soon as that happens, Corsi will be calling on me to hold up my end of the deal, and I'm not ready to marry Rialta. I need more time to figure out a plan.

9
RI

His fingers rake through my hair before he balls my hair into a fist and yanks back hard. His lips crash down on mine before I can cry out—mixing the pain and pleasure just the way I like it.

"You have to be quiet, baby. We can't wake anyone. We can't get caught," he says.

He's right; this is forbidden. It's wrong, but that doesn't mean I can control the sounds leaving my body, not when his fingers are slipping down my body between my legs. One pinch of my clit between his fingers, and I'm screaming again. The only thing keeping us from getting caught is his mouth pressed down tightly over mine.

I shouldn't want to get caught; I really shouldn't. But doing this while it's forbidden somehow makes it all so much hotter. I want to see how far we can push this.

We're currently hiding beneath the covers in the darkness of the night. I want to push us to the limits of our control. I want to drive him so wild with need and desire that he damns the consequences. That's how much I want him to want me; it's how much I want him.

His fingers continue to tease me. He pulls every drop of my wet desire from my body until I'm so close to the edge there is nowhere to go but over it.

He smirks against my lips, knowing how fast he can make me come.

It's okay; I'll give him take this win. It's not really a win for him after all since I get to experience the first of many mind-blowing orgasms. And I'll make sure I win the next round.

Another circle of his finger over my clit, and I come undone—I lose it. I lose my mind to him. I scream. I cry. I go to some otherworldly place where he barely exists in my mind. I explode with pleasure.

When I finally come back down to earth and look at him, his expression is priceless.

"You enjoy that?" he asks, knowingly.

"Yes. Was I too loud?" I grin knowingly as well.

"Never."

His lips start to work their way down my body. But he doesn't get to have all the fun.

I push against his chest, needing to get to my favorite appendage of his between my legs. But damn does he want to kiss down my body; he barely budges.

I push harder—too hard, and suddenly he's a heap on the floor.

I giggle uncontrollably before jumping down on top of his naked body.

"You're ridiculous." He shakes his head.

"And you love me."

He flashes me a bright smile but doesn't say the words. He never says the words, and neither do I. The words are forbidden, given our situation. *How can we love each other when he's promised to another?*

I run my nails down his chest as punishment for not saying the words I'm so desperate to hear. I'll get him to say them. I'll get him to say he loves me so loud it wakes up the world; fuck the consequences.

He seems suspicious of me, but he wants me too badly to resist. *Can he resist not saying he loves me too?*

I'm betting no. I've been disappointed before, but I rarely lose. I'll hear those magic words by the end of the night.

I move my nails down his body until I get to his cock. It's already standing at attention, in desperate need of my touch. I drag my nails up his shaft, lighter than before but still enough to inflict a little pain for not giving me what I want.

He groans, but it's so low I can barely hear it, not loud enough for the house to hear.

"You can moan louder than that," I purr.

Then I lower my mouth over his cock, taking him all in at one time.

He gasps in shock.

I grin around his cock as I deep throat him and then run my tongue up and down his entire length.

His eyes roll back in his head, and his hand fists as he tries to hold onto what little control he has left.

So close, you're so close. Just let go. Give me one last good night. Just one night where you tell me the truth. One where I know you love me for sure. One where we've told each other all the truths, all the lies, and we still love each other.

I just need this once so I can survive a lifetime of not getting him.

That's what I keep telling myself. I only need one time

to know this is completely real. A night of real feelings, not fake, where neither of us is holding back.

He's getting close, starting to lose control, starting to near admitting the truth.

His hand goes to my neck, trying to pull me off him, but I won't stop. I'll give him as many orgasms as I can tonight. This is just the first of many—the night is still young. Every orgasm I pull from him is a chance for him to admit the truth.

His growl is loud, ruthless, and powerful when he comes deep in my mouth—his warm, salty cum spills down my throat.

I release him, licking my lips as I do.

He breathes hard and fast. He was loud but still far too quiet.

His eyes open, locking on mine in worry.

But I'm not even close to being done with him.

I stand up and extend my hand to him, helping him to his feet.

But before I realize what he's doing, he tackles me onto the bed. My legs are spread wide, and his head is staring hungrily between them.

I hold my breath, knowing another orgasm is going to be the death of me. He knows it too. I guess I'll die from too strong a release.

Without warning, he dives between my legs, holding them open while his tongue devours me in delicious strokes. I'm so fucking sensitive already, and he's so damn good at what he does. I'm seeing stars way too soon.

And yet, he still hasn't said the words I'm desperate to hear. I might never get those words again. I might just have to accept this feeling—him worshipping my body like he loves me—may be the best I get.

"Beckett!" I yell as me makes me come again. "Beckett, Beckett, Beckett!"

"River!" I feel hands shaking my body, and I hear him speak, but I don't understand. "Ri! Wake up, Ri."

More shaking against my shoulders before I finally open my eyes. Beckett is over me, but he's not smiling like he should be. In fact, he's frowning.

Maybe I was too loud. Maybe I woke up the others. Maybe they know we still love each other. Maybe I did what was forbidden.

I don't say anything as he stares down at me with a mix of anger and confusion on his face. I look past his face and find him dressed.

I, on the other hand, am not. I'm in bed, covered in sweat, and I reek of sex. My hand is firmly between my legs, coated with my cum.

It takes me a minute to piece together what just happened. I had a sex dream about Beckett. None of it was real.

But now he's here.

Why is he in my room looking like a fucking god? A furious, hot god, but a god all the same.

Oh yea, probably because I called out his name.

"Something you want to tell me?" he asks.

I shake my head. "Nope."

I feel my cheeks heating. I'm sure they are a bright red shade of red. And I'm pretty sure he knows exactly what I was dreaming about.

"Are you okay?" he asks, his voice dropping, almost as if he understands, and he genuinely wants to make sure

I'm okay. He's not scolding me for having the dreams. He's not upset that he's going to have to come up with some weird excuse to explain why I called out his name in my sleep to Rialta.

"I'm fine," I reply.

I'm anything but fine. I've been trapped in this nightmare for less than twenty-four hours, and I'm already failing.

He nods. His eyes roll down my bare chest, stopping where my nipples stick out from the top of the covers.

I grab the covers and lift them to cover my naked chest.

He turns his head to the floor next to my bed. I follow his gaze and find my clothes tossed haphazardly on the carpet.

He turns his attention back to me. He doesn't say a word, but he knows. God, he fucking knows exactly what I dreamed about.

He leans forward, taking a deep breath.

"What are you doing?" I ask.

Silently he lifts my right fingers to his mouth before wrapping his lips around them and sucking them clean.

It's fucking hot, seeing him lick my cum from my fingers. But it's also wrong, so fucking wrong. It feels like he participated in my sordid dream in the only way he could.

A second later, he turns and leaves the room without a word.

The second he's gone, I lift the covers over my head, like that will somehow ease my embarrassment and make things better.

Damn, damn, damn.

I want to scream, but I don't want to draw any more attention to myself.

I fucked up. I can't keep letting Beckett think I still want him. I can't give him any reason to doubt that he should be trying to fall in love with the real Rialta, not me. I'm a nobody. I'm an heir to no kingdom. I have no real money. I have no future except to protect the one woman I love as my sister.

And now, thanks to my stupid dream and stupid comment yesterday when I was tending to his finger, he thinks I care about him. Now I'm going to have to work twice as hard to convince him otherwise.

I throw the covers down and put my clothes back on, knowing I need to make an appearance out of my room sooner than later. And if I'm going to do my job, I need to go check in on Rialta.

I step out into the living room, but any worries about what happened in the bedroom are gone as soon as I see Beckett and Rialta together. They're sitting together on the couch, facing each other. Beckett has his arm around the back of the cushions, inches away from touching Rialta.

Worst of all, they're laughing—full out, hearty laughs. Beckett isn't faking either. They're real laughs.

"I would not like Die Hard; you're crazy," Rialta says.

"Tonight, we are watching it. No more of that bridesmaid shit."

"It was a great movie!"

"How would you know? You fell asleep five minutes into it," he replies.

Rialta opens her mouth to reply but laughs, having no comeback.

Beckett raises his eyebrows. "That's what I thought."

I walk past them, neither of them looking at me as I make my way to the kitchen. They have goo-goo eyes for each other, like two teenagers flirting with each other for the first time. It makes me sick.

No, this is a good thing. This is what I want. I want Beckett to like her and Rialta to like him. Just because I'm jealous doesn't mean anything.

I grab a mug and pour myself a stale cup of coffee.

Now what?

I can still hear them giggling together on the couch. Rialta is clearly fine. I pull out my phone to check the security cameras and any alerts from last night, but there is nothing.

"You stink!" I hear Rialta laugh again.

"So do you," Beckett retorts.

"Not as bad as you. You shower first. I can't stand the smell of you a second longer."

"Fine," Beckett grumbles. I hear him pad to the tiny bathroom, and I try to keep my thoughts from how good it felt to be in there with him yesterday. I wait until I hear the door close and the water turn on for good measure before making my way to the living room.

"Oh, River, you're awake," Rialta says with a bright smile.

I smile at her, too, knowing she doesn't mean anything by her comment at not noticing me, even though I walked right past her. She's just oblivious to the world sometimes.

"Did you sleep well?" I ask as I take up the Beckett's spot on the couch. I quickly realize how close they really were to one another once I sit down.

"I did, thanks to Beckett."

"You're starting to fall for him?" I ask with a knowing smile.

Rialta shrugs. "He's a nice guy, that's all. I'm trying to

get to know him. I wouldn't say I'm falling. I don't fall that easily."

My eyebrows shoot up, and I cough on my coffee. "Really? I seem to remember a girl who would fall for every guy. That was sort of the problem."

She laughs. "Maybe you're right. But you picked this one for me, so I can't go wrong this time, can I?"

I have nothing to say to that, so I just sip my coffee.

"You feeling okay?"

She nods tightly. "Just on edge after what happened. I still can't believe it."

"I know, I'm sorry. I'll make sure security—"

"It's not your fault. You did your job. It was the others who failed. That's part of the problem. You and father are the only ones I can trust." She pauses. "Well, now Beckett too."

Rialta studies my expression. "I can trust Beckett too, right?" she asks.

I nod. "Yes, no matter what happens, you can trust him. He's added you to his list of people he cares about, so yes, you can trust him."

"I have three people in my life I can trust; that's enough. I don't want anyone else on my security team—just you and Beckett."

"Rialta, I don't think that's a good idea. We need more people, or what happened yesterday could have been so much worse."

She shakes her head. "No. It's because of the others there was a problem. From now on, it's just the three of us."

Great...

The bathroom door opens, and Beckett steps out. We both turn, and I freeze. Beckett is standing, still dripping wet, in the tiniest towel I've ever seen wrapped around his waist, barely covering anything. He looks grumpy from the crappy arrangement until he sees my expression. Then he lights up like he couldn't have planned this better himself.

I look over at Rialta, and she's practically drooling at the sight of him. Maybe he's lighting up because of the way she's looking at him. He's happy his future wife finds him so attractive.

He is a very attractive man, even with his clothes on, but his nakedness takes it to another level. His muscles are built, the kind any hot-blooded woman wants to run her tongue over. He has a very defined V that cuts down beneath the towel. And there is a beautiful tattoo in the center of his chest. One that is most definitely going to have to change now that he belongs to the Corsi mafia and not the Retribution Kings.

He's absolutely beautiful.

I look over at Rialta, and she only has lust-filled eyes for him.

I know he's always concerned about what people think about his missing arm. But somehow, even the residual limb is all muscle and makes him even more attractive. He's a man that would risk everything for the woman he loves. It's built into his DNA, into every part of him. And he's going to be that man for Rialta.

"Eww, put on some clothes, Beckett," Rialta teases him. But the way she bats her eyes at him and licks her lips tells him exactly what she would do to him if I weren't here.

"I would, but I don't have any clean clothes," he says. When he speaks, he speaks to her, but he's looking at me.

"I packed a few things in a suitcase for everyone before we came. I left the suitcase in the car. I'll go get it," I say.

I hop off the couch so fast you'd think it was on fire. I

take my time getting the suitcase, hating that I'm going to have to go back into the house and face them.

Thank god, at least I don't have a cock that can get hard and give me away at a time like this. Although, Beckett knows me well enough to know when I'm turned on.

Fuck, I'm not going to survive this.

10

BECKETT

I slip the black T-shirt that River packed for me over my head, hitting my elbow on the wall in the cramped bathroom. I curse as a jolt of pain radiates down my arm. I bite down and end up biting my tongue, spilling blood into my mouth, and causing more pain.

"Fuck," I groan a little louder than I probably should.

I hate it here, not just because this bathroom is tiny and the cramped house keeps finding small ways to injure me. I hate it because my heart is literally being tortured.

I'm so close to River, and yet, I can't touch her.

I wasn't sure if she wanted me. She even told me everything was an act. She was just doing her job, finding the best man for her sister. But that's not what it seems like.

River looks at me with a deep lust in her eyes. She watches me even when she should be watching Rialta. She worries about me. She tries to push me away but fails at every chance. And then this morning, she had a sex dream about me.

If it's just lust, then I'll give her up and marry Rialta. I'll save my family and learn to be a good Corsi leader. But if it's more than just lust, if it's love or something like love, then I have to know.

Because I'll...I don't know what I'll do, but I'm not sure I can give River up if she loves me too.

I spit blood into the sink, rinse the sink clean, and then stride back out into the living room. I plan on getting under River's skin to see how she reacts, but all I find is Rialta sitting on the couch alone.

"Where's Ri? I mean River." I'm still not getting used to calling her River. I'll probably always think of her as Ri, but Ri can just as easily be a nickname for Rialta as it is for River.

"She went for a run," Rialta says.

I raise my eyebrows. "A run? I thought she's supposed to stay here and protect you?"

Rialta grins. "Worried about me? Don't worry; River is keeping me safe. She's checking the grounds for signs of anyone. The security system is armed, and she left me here with you. She said I should trust you as much as her, so I'm perfectly safe."

I'm sure that's why she left, to check for intruders, not to get away from me. Her cheeks have been a bright red since I found her touching herself in her bed as she called out my name. She left because she's too chicken shit to face me.

I plop down on the couch next to Rialta. She looks at me schemingly. I can see her wheels turning with an idea.

"What are you thinking?" I ask.

"You know you're going to have to get rid of that tattoo before we get married."

It's the first time she's mentioned our wedding since our first ceremony resulted in her fainting. I almost choke on my saliva at how casually she said that like it was a forlorn conclusion.

"I do," I say. But whether thankfully or unfortunately, Corsi hasn't found and ensured the safety of my family yet, so the wedding can be held off for a little bit longer.

Her eyes glow mischievously.

"I don't like that look," I say.

She shrugs. "Get used to it. It's one of my favorite looks."

"You seem to be feeling better."

"I am. I can thank your excellent soup and caretaking skills for my speedy recovery," she says.

I shake my head. "I don't think I can take any of the credit. That's all you, but I'm just glad you're feeling better."

Even if no one will tell me why you fell ill in the first place.

The front door opens, and a sweaty River stands in the doorway. Her hair is pulled up in a high messy bun, her white shirt is covered in sweat, and her black leggings have sweat stains on them. She really pushed herself on her run to get that sweaty, probably trying to forget something.

She's panting hard when she enters but keeps her eyes on Rialta. She doesn't even acknowledge my presence. "How are you feeling?" she asks Rialta.

"Better than you," Rialta teases.

River playfully hits Rialta on the shoulder. "I'm fine, just out of shape."

"Or you pushed yourself too much because you're worried about something?" Rialta muses.

I agree with Rialta and turn my attention to River to see how she'll answer.

"I'm going to shower," River says through gasps for air.

"Perfect, then we can go," Rialta says, stopping River in her tracks.

"Go where exactly?" she asks.

"The closest tattoo shop. Beckett needs his tattoo fixed."

River looks at me with a glare.

"Don't look at me; this wasn't my idea," I say, throwing my arm behind the couch so I can watch the show that is their argument.

I'm still figuring out how the two of them interact together. It seems Rialta takes the role of a typical younger, spoiled sister who always gets what she wants. River takes on the responsible, older sister role, who can't say no to the younger, but I know River wants to keep Rialta safe too.

River snaps her head back to Rialta. "I'm not sure that's safe. No one knows we're here, but if we venture into town, it will be harder to hide. Beckett can get his tattoo fixed later."

"I'm not going to hide away the rest of my life. I've tried that, and it wasn't any fun. I trust the two of you to keep me safe. Nothing will change after we're married. The three of us will live together, keeping each other safe, but I will not be locked away in a tower for the rest of my life. I'd rather live," Rialta says.

"The three of us will live together?" I ask.

"Yes, River will live with us as our exclusive bodyguard after we get married. I don't trust anyone but her, not even our father's men. She will be with us always."

River won't make eye contact with me, but I know it's true. We're expected to live together after Rialta and I are married. I've never thought of myself as one who would ever cheat once I make a vow, but with temptation that close, it's going to be near impossible for me to keep any wedding vows to Rialta. All the more reason this can't be the plan. If I do agree to marry Rialta, I'll be faithful to her, even if it kills me.

"Rialta, I know you want some freedom, but you have just started healing. Do you really think you're ready for a trip?" River tries reasoning with her.

"We're going. I'm in charge, and we're going. You can arrange the logistics. You decide the when and where and how, but we're going," Rialta stands and stomps off to her bedroom, slamming the door shut like a teenager demanding to out on a Friday night.

I look to River, who just shrugs. She's not going to argue with Rialta about it.

"We'll be safe about it. Wait until night to go. Find a tattoo shop hidden in the small town. It will be fine," I say.

River bites her bottom lip. "Nothing is ever safe and fine when it comes to Rialta. The bigger question is, why does she want to go so badly? Is this all really just about a tattoo?"

And before I can answer her, River heads into the bathroom and closes the door, leaving me wondering.

What is Rialta really up to?

We pull up to a suburban tattoo parlor a little after nine. We're not too close to the city, but also the town is not so small that anyone that sees us will be able to easily recall us since they get so few visitors.

River parks along the street about a block away from the parlor, and we all climb out of the car. Rialta immediately walks over to me, grabbing my arm like we're already a couple.

"So, what do you want to get to cover your tattoo?" Rialta asks.

I shrug. "It doesn't really matter to me, whatever the artist recommends."

"Really? So they could recommend getting a pink bunny to cover up that tattoo, and you'd be fine with it?"

"As long as the crown tattoo is gone, I'll be happy. If a big pink bunny tattoo is the best way to do that, then so be it. Although, I doubt that's going to be the best way to cover it up."

She laughs. "Probably not. Will you let me pick the tattoo then?"

"Sure," I say.

Rialta lights up and bounces as we walk to the tattoo shop. But I can't help but notice River's reaction. She trails behind us like a third wheel, listening carefully to our conversation. Perhaps the best way to learn River's true feelings is to act like I'm interested in Rialta. I should stop flirting with River and give Rialta all my attention to see if she cracks. That's my new plan.

I pull Rialta tighter against me as we walk to the front door.

"Shit, it's closed," Rialta says, slamming us to a halt.

"Darn. Oh, well, I guess we should head back," River says from behind us, almost like she planned for the shop to be closed.

"Or..." Rialta looks to River. "You could pick the lock."

"No," River says, turning around.

Rialta lets go of my arm and chases after River. She grabs her arm. "Please."

I can't make out Rialta's face, but I'm sure she's pouting

and batting her eyelashes, pulling out all the stops to get River to help.

River sighs.

"Please," Rialta begs again.

"Fine." River walks past Rialta and toward the front door where I'm still standing. "Stand guard and let me know if anyone is coming," River says to me.

I raise my eyebrows. "You're really going to break into this tattoo shop?"

She rolls her eyes. "Like this is the worst thing I've done."

I pull Rialta to my side, afraid she's using this as a distraction to run off. I don't want to spend my night chasing a young woman.

"It's open," River says a couple of seconds later.

"That was fast. I'm impressed," Rialta says.

"You severely underestimate my skills if you thought that was going to take me very long," River says.

We all walk inside. None of us turn the lights on in case we draw attention to ourselves. The street is quiet, and there aren't many people out tonight, so us being in here shouldn't be a problem.

"We're in here, but one little problem. None of us are tattoo artists, so I don't know how you plan on covering my tattoo with another," I say.

River folds her arms across her chest as she looks to Rialta, waiting for her to answer.

"Well, I thought I'd do it," Rialta says.

River grins.

"Do you, uh, have any experience doing tattoos?" I rub the back of my neck nervously.

"No, I've never given a tattoo before."

"Then what makes you think you can give me a tattoo?

Not only give me a tattoo but cover up the one I currently have?"

"My sketches are quite good, and I'm a fast learner. I can't imagine drawing and giving a tattoo is much different." Rialta grins at me, almost daring me to say no.

I spot River out of the corner of my eye, almost cracking up at the thought of letting Rialta tattoo me.

But we came all this way, and I'm not one to back down. If Rialta wants to give me a tattoo, then she can give me a tattoo.

I grab my shirt and pull it off over my head. "Go for it. You'll be the one that has to look at it every time I fuck you, so it'll be your fault if you screw it up."

Rialta gasps.

River freezes.

Now I'm the one smirking at the two of them.

"So, are we doing this or not?" I ask.

"Oh, we are definitely doing this," Rialta answers before walking into one of the rooms.

I follow after her.

"I'm going to stay out here to make sure we're not spotted," River says, staying in the lobby.

I frown, but I know I'm getting under her skin. Soon enough, I'll get River to talk to me.

Right now, I have to turn my attention to Rialta and her skills with a tattoo gun.

Rialta is standing next to a flattened chair. She taps it happily, waiting for me to lie down so she can go to work.

"I can't believe I'm doing this," I grumble under my breath.

She grins happily. "I can be very persuasive."

"Yea, that's it." This plan has nothing to do with me

trying to drive the woman waiting in the lobby crazy with need for me.

I lie on the table and stare up at the bare ceiling while Rialta goes through the supplies and figures out what she needs. Before I know it, she's leaning over me, looking me in the eyes.

"Do you trust me?" she asks, looking sincere and heartfelt.

That's what this is to her—a moment of trust. She needs me to trust her as she trusts me.

She holds the tattoo gun in her hand. She drew no stencil. She hasn't done any practice runs with the gun. This is going to be a disaster, and yet, when I look into her eyes, I do have faith in her—far more faith in her than I probably should.

"Yes, I trust you," I reply.

"Good, don't move."

Slowly, she lowers the tattoo gun to my chest. The familiar prick of the needle and buzzing of pain lull me into a trance.

Rialta's tongue sticks out of her mouth, and her brows furrow as she concentrates on what she's doing. She doesn't talk or even look at me.

I close my eyes as she works, taking a short nap and feeling calmer than I have in days with her working on the tattoo on my chest. I'm not even sure I care what it turns into; I'm just happy for this peaceful experience.

"Beckett," I hear her soft voice.

I open my eyes, and Rialta is grinning down at me. "I'm finished. Want to see it before I bandage it?"

I nod, although maybe it would be better if I never saw it.

She holds out her hand to me and helps me off the

chair. There is a full-length mirror in the corner of the room. I take a deep breath, preparing myself for anything before I look up.

My eyes pop wide, and my mouth falls open as I stare at myself in the mirror. I can't believe what I'm seeing, and I can't believe that Rialta isn't a certified tattoo artist that does this for a living. It's incredible; it really is.

I wouldn't call it a cover-up; it's more of an addition to the original tattoo. A second crown fit for a princess has been added. Details on both crowns make them look like they were done at the same time. It's very clear that the two are meant to be equals—equal strengths, equal in power, equal in love.

"River! Come look!" Rialta shouts giddily.

I'm not sure if River is going to come, but a moment later, she appears at the door. She doesn't come close enough to see all the intricate details, but she can see what the tattoo has become. She can see the additional crown.

"It's beautiful. You're very talented, Rialta," she says, forcing her words to grow louder than the whisper she started speaking in.

"Thank you, I know," Rialta says proudly.

"It really is amazing," I agree as River walks back out of the room.

Rialta takes my hand. "You really like it?"

"I do. I really do."

I study the crown closer, and I see the name etched across it—Ri.

Ri for Rialta or Ri for River?

I want to ask Rialta what she meant or if she forgot to finish the name on the crown, but I'm terrified of her answer.

She helps me cover the tattoo with petroleum jelly and

a bandage to protect it. But that doesn't stop me from remembering every line of the tattoo and River's face when she saw it. She was in awe of how beautiful it looked but hated what she thought it represented—Rialta and me.

I'm not sure what it represents yet. I'm not sure if Rialta did it intentionally, keeping it open to both of us, or if she just ran out of room to fit her entire name. I'm not sure Rialta even realizes there's a connection between River and me. If she did, would she still want to marry me?

We leave the tattoo shop and head back to the house, returning with more questions than answers.

11

RI

I force my feet to move faster. Faster and faster and faster until my body can barely keep up with my feet. The wind beats at my face, and my heart struggles to pump enough blood through my body to keep me going. My lungs burn, and my legs feel numb from running so hard.

My foot slips on uneven pavement, and I fall to the ground, my wrists catching my weight. I pant hard into the ground, knowing I can't keep doing this to myself every day. I have to face reality.

My reality is the man I love is falling for my best friend. I'm going to have to get used to seeing them together every day. I need to adjust to thinking of them as a couple. Rip off the bandaid and just deal with the pain—the sooner I do that, the sooner this ache in my chest will start to heal.

Last night damn near killed me, though. Listening to the sound of the tattoo gun, knowing she was marking his skin permanently. She was repeatedly touching his chest. He put his complete trust in her. It was too much for me to handle.

And then when Rialta called me in there to see the work she did, and I saw the crown she added to represent her...I lost it. I wanted to cry, to scream, to throw something, but I couldn't because Beckett isn't mine. He never was. He was always hers.

It only got worse on the drive home. I drove while Beckett and Rialta flirted the whole way back, talking about everything from their favorite foods to movies to sex positions. I wish I had headphones to block them out, something I'll definitely remember to carry with me from now on.

And then, when we got back, they immediately went to her bedroom together.

TOGETHER!

I just stared frozen from the front door for a few minutes, waiting for Beckett to come back out. He had to be just tucking her in and making sure she had everything she needed for the night, right? But after thirty minutes of me just staring at the door, it became obvious he wasn't leaving that room.

I eventually walked to my bedroom and saw their lights were, in fact, off, but I could hear them on the other side of the door. I don't know if it was my overactive imagination or reality, but I swear I heard them kissing and moaning together.

I ran into my room, slammed my door, and wore headphones the rest of the night. But I didn't sleep.

I just kept playing images of the two of them together in my head. Of their wedding. Of them kissing in front of me. Of him carrying her up the stairs of their brand new house to go fuck her in every room and on every surface. Of the day she finds out she's pregnant.

It all played like a horror movie in my head. Every

piece of their perfect life, with me by their side, watching and protecting and enduring it all.

I push myself off the ground and wipe the dirt on the sides of my leggings. But this is what my entire life has been for. This is what I wanted. I wanted to give Rialta her happily ever after. She deserves it after the life she's lived.

But don't I deserve it too?

I don't answer that. I don't compare my life to Rialta's. We've both been through a lot. The difference between her and me is that I know I'm strong enough to handle anything. Rialta is strong too, but she doesn't believe in her strength—not yet, at least. I know I'm strong enough. And like I've endured countless pains before, I'll endure losing Beckett.

I take my time walking back to the house, hoping the happy couple is awake and hopefully not too into public displays of affection this morning. At least, I hope they won't kiss and get all handsy when I'm around.

Maybe I should have some rules about what they can and can't do around me? If they want me to continue to be their security guard, that's the least they could do.

I open the door, and, to my relief, they are both dressed. Rialta is sitting on the couch, and Beckett is in the kitchen. They aren't kissing. They aren't even touching.

"Have a good run?" Rialta asks.

"Yep." I don't give her any details of what I've been thinking or any rules I might need them to abide by, not yet. The truth is I want them both to be happy, and if being together makes them happy, then I can be happy for them.

Maybe.
Eventually.
I'm working on it.

I sigh.

"I'm going to shower, but what's the plan for today? Movie day? Going for a walk? Baking some sugary treat?" I walk toward the bathroom.

Beckett walks back into the living room, carrying two thermoses of what I assume is coffee. He looks to Rialta, waiting for her to speak. It seems the plans for today have been decided without me.

"Actually..." Rialta runs her hands through her dark brown hair before twirling the ends around her fingers nervously.

I look to Beckett, seeing if he will give anything away, but he's stone-faced.

"Actually, what?" I ask.

"Actually, Beckett and I need some time alone. We are going to have lunch together."

"You're going to have lunch together where? I can drive you and keep a lookout outside the restaurant. Some places will be safer than others."

"No, we—just Beckett and I—are going to have lunch. We are going to drive ourselves. You can have the day off," Rialta says with barely-mustered confidence.

"The day off?" I raise an eyebrow. I haven't had a day off since I took this job when I was five. I don't even know what a day off means.

"Yes, a day off. I know this place isn't that glamorous, and there isn't much to do, but you can watch and movies, eat any of the food Beckett cooked, take a nap, go for a walk, whatever you like," Rialta says.

I frown and look to Beckett. "Are you okay with this? You'll do whatever it takes to keep her safe?"

Beckett looks me dead in the eyes, but I still can't read

him, not really. "Yes, I'll keep Rialta safe; you have my word."

Then he walks over to where Rialta is seated. She stands, taking one of the thermoses from underneath his arm, and then hooks her arm through his.

"When will you be back?" I ask, still not sure I should let them out of my sight. What would Vincent say?

I don't work for Vincent, not anymore. I work for Rialta.

They walk toward the door. "Before midnight," Rialta grins.

I roll my eyes. She always loved Cinderella.

Then they're gone, and I'm left alone in the tiny house, clueless if I've just been played and they're never coming back.

Worst yet, I'm pretty sure this is the moment I've been dreading. This is when they talk and agree to get married if they aren't disappearing to go elope right now. This is the moment they fall in love. This is the moment my heart shatters completely.

I sink to my knees on the floor as tears begin to fall. I could still stop them. I could go after them. Tell Beckett the truth—I love him, and I can't give him up.

But I won't. I can't. My entire life would be for nothing if I did.

I don't regret falling in love with him. No matter how much this hurts, I won't regret that. Loving him has reminded me that even though I am nothing more than a protector and a guard, I should find something I love beyond my work, and I deserve to be loved. And I'll find that love again.

12

BECKETT

RIALTA and I rush to the car to get away from that awkward exchange with River as soon as possible.

"So, where are we going?" I ask as soon as I'm settled in the driver's seat.

Rialta looks around. "Somewhere far enough that River can't see us, but close enough that we can come back if we need to in a hurry. Just somewhere nice to have a picnic."

I back out of the driveway and head down the gravel road until the house is no longer visible. I spot a nearby small hill overlooking much of the fields around and decide it would be a good spot to have lunch.

"You shouldn't have worried River like that," I scold as we drive.

Rialta looks at me with sad eyes. "I know, but it was necessary."

"Why?" I turn to look at her as I bring the car to a stop.

She shakes her head and gets out.

I follow suit, taking our thermoses from the car's center console. Rialta opens a back door where she pulls out a bag of sandwiches and fruit she packed out along with a blanket for us to sit on. Then we march up the small hill, spread out the blanket, and arrange our picnic.

We eat our sandwiches and drink our coffee, the whole time I'm burning with questions for her, but I resist. I remain patient, waiting to see if this is the moment she talks openly with me.

"Thank you for not asking," she says, finally.

I look up at her, almost dropping my thermos of coffee in my lap. I swallow hard, waiting to hear something of the truth, something of the pieces I've been missing.

"Did you know I'm not an only child?" she asks.

I shake my head. I'm guessing most of what I'm about to find out I don't know or I know very little about.

"I have an older brother and older sister—well, had," she says sadly.

I want to apologize for her loss, but it's best I remain quiet and let her talk. I don't want to scare her, and I'm pretty sure the only reason she's talking now is because I've given her so much space.

"My brother died when he was still a baby. My sister made it to three before she was killed, along with my mother."

My eyes widen. I had no idea she had siblings.

"We never figured out who killed them. If it was an internal job, someone who worked for my father, or one of our enemies wanting to see the Corsi mafia end and my father suffer as much as possible."

She takes a deep breath.

"I was just a baby when my sister and mother died. After that, my father never let me out of his sight," she continues.

I can understand his need for control after losing so

many close to him. I wouldn't let her out of my sight either. But even that doesn't guarantee her protection; it doesn't guarantee her life.

"We were at a playground one day. I loved the slides. My father would spend hours with me at that playground, helping me up the stairs and then catching me going down the slide. He was amazing like that.

"But on one particular day, he got a phone call. He wasn't at the bottom of the slide when I came down. A strange man I'd never met was. My father was only gone a second, but it was enough for the man to shoot me once in the stomach."

Rialta lifts her shirt, revealing a scar to the left of her belly button.

"I don't know why I didn't blackout, but I didn't. My father came running, phone to his ear. He was already on the phone calling for an ambulance and probably calling on all of the mafia to find the man and kill him for what he did. As he was running across the parking lot, a girl found me first. She was maybe a year or two older than me if that—dark long hair and big deep eyes that held more wisdom than my frail body understood.

"Without hesitation, that girl took off her sweatshirt and applied pressure to my wound. She talked to me and told me it was going to be okay. She kept me awake by asking me all sorts of questions like my favorite color, favorite toy, and if I had any siblings. She kept me talking. She kept me conscious."

Rialta smiles. "That girl saved my life. When my father approached, he froze when he saw me. He thankfully had already called an ambulance, but when he saw me injured, he just froze. He couldn't help me. The pain and trauma overwhelmed him. But that little girl, she could help."

"River," I say, already knowing it was her.

She nods. "Yes, River saved my life that day. She stopped the bleeding until the paramedics got there. My father wasn't sure what to do. The girl was at the park by herself, and she was the only witness to what happened. So my father told her to get in our car with him, and together they followed my ambulance to the hospital. I'm pretty sure River asked him a million questions too, and that kept him from having a complete breakdown. She saved him too."

She saved her. She saved him. She saved me. *River saves people, but who saves her?*

"After that, River never left my bed in the hospital. We became best friends. We were inseparable. We shared everything together, and most of all, we helped each other heal. River grew up in foster care. She never knew who her parents were. And at the time, her foster father was beating and neglecting her. So she was more than happy to spend all of her time with me, even though Father rarely let me out of his sight."

I curse under my breath. They both went through so much.

"The attacks on my life kept coming. None were as close to succeeding as that first one, but they were enough to scare my father after what he'd been through. We rarely left the house. River started tasting my food before I ate it to make sure it wasn't poisoned. If I had to go to the doctor for an appointment, River would dress up as me and go out with one of the guards as a diversion." Rialta looks down like she's disgusted by what her father did and the risk River took even though she was only a child.

"There was a second bad attack. My wound had only just healed, and Father was afraid of his own shadow. He couldn't think straight. I was kidnapped, taken right under his nose," she goes on.

Rialta looks out at the vastness in front of us. She is speechless for a few minutes, most likely reliving whatever horrors happened to her while she was kidnapped. It's not my place to ask. If it helps her to share the memories, then she will. If not, then I don't need to know.

"It was horrible. It took my father three days to find me. When he did, he'd had enough. He wasn't going to take any more chances. He wasn't going to lose the last of his family." She wraps her arms around her chest in a hug. I would offer to hug her myself, but I'm not sure she'd want that.

"He sent me away to live with strangers, people outside this dangerous world. He wouldn't contact them or me until I turned twenty-one. Until I was old enough to reclaim my title and place in the mafia. Until I was old enough to marry and bear children. He hoped he could unearth the people responsible for all the attacks before then, but he never did. He never figured it out. He never came to get me."

"Until now," I say.

She nods. "All that time, River pretended to be me. He told her I was dead. Then he slowly trained her and hypnotized her to make her think she was actually me. Father only told one other person—Kek. He turned her into me. He took her out of foster care, although I don't think he ever technically adopted her. He got her out of that bad situation, gave her a future, but it was a future that was never truly hers."

She looks at me with tears in her eyes. "Father knew

she was stronger than me. He knew she could survive when I couldn't in this world. He chose her, and she agreed."

Tears fall now, and I can't stand to not hold her. I move closer slowly, so slowly it's almost painful, waiting for any sign of her pushing me away, but I find none.

I hold my arm out to her, waiting to see if she wants to be held. She falls into my shoulder, and I wrap my arm around her, letting her cry.

"I'm a horrible person. I let River risk her life, her entire fucking life, for me," she wails.

"No, you're not horrible. Your father made that choice, not you. You were just a kid. And River was happy to take on the role. She played the role well."

Too well.

"She should have stayed Rialta and let me go live elsewhere. I shouldn't have come back," she says.

"Why? What do you mean?"

"The wedding. One of the guards handed me a glass of wine before the wedding, and I drank it without question. That's why I passed out. That's why my heart stopped. That's why they pumped my stomach. I was poisoned."

"That's not your fault," I say.

"In the years I've been gone, River has successfully avoided being poisoned, or shot, or kidnapped."

"Well, that's just not true. All of those things have happened to her too. She survived them, same as you."

"She's stronger. She should be Rialta Corsi."

I frown. "She's only stronger because she's been trained her whole life to be. No one can be Rialta Corsi better than you. You know why?" I put my finger under her chin, lifting it. "Because you are the only Rialta Corsi. And she's the only River Corsi. You are both strong ass women who can defeat anyone. You are stronger than this. You both are."

She leans into my chest. "I don't feel that way. I feel weak."

"That's because you're still recovering. You're still figuring out who you are after pretending to be someone else for so long. But I'll be by your side, and so will River. Together we will figure out how to survive this and accomplish whatever goals you set. We will figure out how to get your strength back."

She nods into my shoulder.

I hold her for a long time, so long that the sun begins to set and a chill creeps over us. We both needed the time to process everything she said.

Where has she been this whole time? What was her life like? Did she have a good life before she was brought here? I have a million questions, but she's spilled so many secrets today that I can't possibly ask anything just to satisfy my own curiosity.

We need to get back to the house soon, so we don't freeze to death and keep worrying River. I can't wait any longer to ask the most necessary question, though.

"So why marry me? You came back to reclaim who you are. Why marry a man you barely know, someone your father orders you to marry?" I ask.

"For one, the mafia won't accept a female as their leader. My father won't live forever, and he needs an heir."

"So find someone on your own, someone you could love. Find your match in every way. You're a beautiful, intelligent, strong woman. You'll be able to find a man easily."

"You're someone I could love," she says in almost a whisper.

I suck in a breath. I don't know how I can respond to that. She's someone I could love too if it wasn't for my heart already belonging to another. But it's not going to be helpful to tell her that.

"Besides, I don't just need a good husband. I need a man who is strong and brave and fearless. I need a man who is fair but also a bit ruthless. A man who can take over the mafia, not a fairytale prince who can fall in love with me."

She's right. I still think she could find that man on her own, but I don't say anything.

"War is breaking out everywhere, or so I've been told. Order is needed. The Corsi mafia needs to regain power. They need to be feared once again. Our marriage could end so much death," she says.

"I don't see how us getting married solves anything."

She grins. "That's because you've never held real power before. You've never had the power of the mafia behind you. My father has done a lot of things right, but recently, he's made a lot of mistakes. He doesn't have the full support of the mafia. They're looking for new leadership—fresh, young blood willing to change things while also keeping with their traditions. They want to see that my father has arranged a marriage for me and married me off. That is the mafia way, after all."

"I'm not mafia, though. I'm not sure they'll accept me."

"They will. They've seen you fight in the games. They've seen how fearless you are. You're the brother of Enzo Black. They fear that and respect you because of it."

I nod, understanding. There is no way out of this. I'm going to have to marry her to save my family, to end the war, to protect Rialta.

I just hope I can find a way to free River in the process.

It's not fair to her to stay our main protection. River has given enough, and I know she still loves me. I have to stop trying to get her to admit it. I need her to let me go, so I can let her go. I need to break her heart completely once and for all so she'll leave and restart her own life.

"We also have to get married for her," she says.

I snap my head to Rialta, not understanding.

"River has given everything for this. She's literally given up her childhood through young adulthood. She risked her life. Everything she's been through, she went through to protect me. To protect my future. To give me a life once I came back. To ensure I was well protected by my husband. We have to get married—only then can she be free," Rialta says.

I stare at her, the truth of her words sinking in. We have to get married.

Rialta pulls back to look completely at me but remains close. My initial reaction is to want to back away because she's too deep in my personal space, but I only unwrap my arm around her shoulders.

She leans in and presses her lips ever so softly against mine. Her lips just barely graze mine. Her bottom lip trembles a little against mine as she kisses me. She's scared to death.

I put my hand over her heart and can feel how wildly it's beating.

"I won't hurt you. You don't need to be afraid of me. You don't need to rush anything you aren't ready for, even after we get married. We'll take everything slowly. And even after we're married, if you want out, I'll find you a way out," I say, wishing I could find one for me too.

She presses her lips harder against mine, deepening the kiss without opening her mouth. I'm thankful for her hesitance because I'm not ready to push anything further than this either. I have no idea how I'm going to be a good husband to her. I can protect her, I can be her hero, but her husband? I don't know how I'm supposed to want her, love her, fuck her.

"I know you won't hurt me, but I can't make the same promise to you," she says.

I stare at her, unsure of what she means. All I know is that I won't put anything past a Corsi, even a woman I've been looking at as meek and timid. I won't underestimate her. If she says she might hurt me, then I'll be ready for it.

13

RI

I TRACKED THEM. I couldn't resist. I have a tracker on the car, but I should have put a damn on tracker on Rialta. The girl is going to be the death of me. If she wants me to protect her, then she has to stop leaving without me.

I watch on my phone, trying to figure out how I'm going to get to them. I need a car. Arranging a rental car out here is going to be a pain in the ass, but I'll do what I have to.

The dot stopped about a mile from here. *Did they run into car trouble?*

If they did, I'm sure Beckett can handle it. Or they can walk back easily. But I can't stand to just sit here inside all day. I need to find out if they're okay. The other possibility is that they've been attacked.

I grab my gun and running shoes, and then I'm out the door. My legs cramp up immediately. I've already run today, and my legs don't want to do it again, but I force them forward.

I run through the empty fields, and then suddenly, I spot them. The car isn't broken down. They haven't been attacked. They just decided to have a damn picnic without telling me that's what they were doing.

I'm going to kill Rialta for doing this to me. Beckett too.

I stop at the bottom of a hill and watch them for a while. They smile at each other. They laugh. And then things turn serious. She's telling him about her past. I'm sure one of them will propose. They'll agree to get married for real this time.

I can't watch that part, so I turn around and run back to the house.

I find a tub of cookie dough ice cream in the freezer and bring it to the couch. I eat my feelings while watching action movies, sparing my heart from any rom-coms right now.

After two movies and an entire pint of ice cream, they still aren't back. I stare at my phone and see they haven't moved from the spot. There's no reason to go looking for them, so I curl up on the couch and wait for them to return.

And wait and wait and wait.

I wish I could sleep. I wish I could run away from this life. I don't know what I'd do, this is the only life I've ever known, but I'd do something different. Become a doctor or lawyer—they both protect people without sacrificing themselves.

Suddenly, the door opens.

I close my eyes tight, not wanting to deal with them tonight. It's late, and I don't want to hear the news. I'm sure I'll be able to face reality with just one more night of sleep.

"Shhh, she's asleep," Rialta says, giggling.

I'm not sure if Beckett believes that or not. He could always see through me.

I squeeze my eyes tighter and slow my breathing, so it appears I'm asleep. But then I hear a sound—the sound of saliva being exchanged.

I should keep my eyes closed. I really shouldn't look, but I like to punish myself. I open my eyes just a sliver, and that's when I see them—kissing.

Both of their eyes are closed, their heads are tilted to deepen the kiss, her tongue pushes deep into his mouth, and his hand rests on her hip.

My heart should be used to breaking by now, but once again, it shatters. There is no denying their feelings are growing, no denying they are falling in love.

Rialta opens her eyes just the slightest as her tongue dips deeper inside his mouth.

I snap my eyes closed, hoping she didn't see me peeking. I don't want her to know that I have feelings for him. He's going to be her husband, not mine. She doesn't need to know I'm madly in love with him. I don't want her to feel any guilt for loving him.

They slowly, painfully, make their way to her bedroom and close the door. Once again, they share the bedroom. I have my headphones ready, so I can ignore what happens once they enter the bedroom.

And once again, I don't sleep.

―――

"You look like hell," Beckett says, standing over me and offering me a cup of coffee.

I sit up and take the coffee. "Thanks."

"Did you sleep at all?"

I avoid answering by sipping my coffee.

"Did you?" I reply.

He grins. "I got excellent sleep, thank you."

"What has you in such a chipper mood this morning?"

"It's time to leave," he says.

I frown. "What does that mean?"

"Lennox texted me early this morning. Corsi found my brother and his family and ensured their safety."

"Oh." I take another sip of my coffee as I process his words. "So that was the deal with Vincent? He protected your family and you…"

"And I marry his daughter," he finishes my heart-breaking sentence.

I nod, my stomach in knots. There was a tiny part of me that hoped the deal he concocted with Vincent had something to do with me, but now I know for sure it didn't. I'm not his family. I'm not the one he loves, not anymore. The bad thing about a man who can fall in love easily is that he can just as easily fall out of love.

I stare at Beckett, and he stares back. There is so much to say between us, so many feelings needing to be taken back. As much as he and Rilata needed an afternoon just to talk, we too need to talk.

I open my mouth to suggest that, even just twenty minutes, when Rialta runs out of the bedroom with a huge smile on her face. Her grin is the kind of smile and dreamy look on her face that says I orgasmed a million times last night.

Kill me, just kill me and put me out of my misery.

"Who is ready for an elopement?!" she squeals, grabbing onto Beckett's arm. She grabs his face and kisses him.

His face is a little shocked at her brazen kiss, but he doesn't resist. He lets her kiss him. I can tell by the bobbing in his throat that he's enjoying it.

They both turn to me.

"Eloping, huh? Congratulations. Are we headed back to a church or—"

"No, we're headed to Las Vegas! That's where you go to get eloped. I never wanted a big church wedding. I always wanted something fun and spontaneous," Rialta says.

I narrow my eyes at her, completely confused. A church wedding with the big princess dress is exactly what she's always wanted. I asked her before we arranged the first wedding. And it's what the mafia would expect of her. It's what Vincent would expect.

I don't know what's changed her mind or if Vincent knows, but I'm guessing he won't care too much as long as they're married.

"Let's go to Vegas then," I say.

14

BECKETT

As RIVER DRIVES and Rialta sleeps against my chest in the backseat, it feels like River is our own personal chauffeur instead of someone special to both of us.

River doesn't seem to mind, though. In fact, I think she'd prefer to keep as much distance between us as possible. If there was a partition in this car, I'm sure she would have happily raised it. As it is, I don't think she's looked in the rearview mirror once. She's definitely avoiding us.

But I'm selfish, and I want her gaze. I want her eyes on me one last time before I get married again. I want all of her. I should be focused on breaking her heart, ripping it to shreds so she can finally start to heal, though.

My own heart is throbbing at the idea. It's wondering how it's supposed to survive too when I long ago gave it to River. If I destroy her heart, I'm destroying my own. My heart isn't meant to survive anyway.

I want nothing but a black hole left in my chest when I'm done. I want River to move on, to forget about me and Rialta and the Corsi mafia. I want her to go find a new life.

I want her to find something that makes her happy because there is nothing left here for her.

Returning my thoughts to my phone, I resume staring at the photo Lennox sent me that shows Enzo, Kai, Langston, Liesel, Zeke, and Siren glaring at the camera. They're clearly not happy, but they're safe on a private jet, ready to take them anywhere in the world. I don't know where they're headed, and I don't want to know; I just want them to be safe, and away from the war my ex-wife started.

We drive all day—River ignoring us, Rialta asleep on my shoulder, and me staring at my family.

We finally pull up to a private airfield. The plan is for us to take a private jet to Vegas. I'm guessing Corsi knows, or we wouldn't have been able to get a plane, and that makes me nervous as hell. It means I can't back out, or he'll put a bullet in my or my family's head.

I'm not sure if Rialta has figured that part out yet.

River stops the car in front of one of the planes she seems to recognize. Finally, she looks in the rearview mirror. Rialta still hasn't woken up. River doesn't say a word, but her eyes tell me everything I need to know. If I don't want to do this, let her know now, and she'll get us out of this, no questions asked.

I think of the photo I've been staring at all day. I think about River. I can't fail either of them; I can't risk any of their lives.

I give a quick shake of my head and lean down toward Rialta to give her a gentle kiss on the forehead, still meeting River's gaze. She gets out of the car and slams the door shut, waking Rialta immediately.

"We're here. You ready for this?" I ask.

Rialta stretches and looks around. "Where's River?"

"She's on the plane already, probably checking it out to make sure it's safe and ready for us."

"Hmmm." I expect Rialta to lean in and kiss me like she has done now about a half dozen times. Each kiss is startling. I have to remind myself each time the kiss is appropriate. I have to remember each kiss is just the beginning of my future. Each kiss is better than kissing Odette, but it's nothing like kissing River.

I brace myself for another kiss I'm going to have to pretend is pleasant, but Rialta opens the door and steps out.

Huh?

I get out after her and retrieve the one packed bag between the three of us from the trunk. We're going to need to get new clothes in Vegas.

I chase Rialta up the jet's stairs. And when I turn into the main cabin, I suddenly wish I could be anywhere else.

While I was expecting that Corsi might make an appearance, I wasn't expecting him, several of his men, and Lennox, Hayes, and Gage.

"We have quite a crowd," I say.

Corsi just looks at me sternly. He doesn't have to speak; I already see the threat in his eyes. If I don't marry Rialta this time, I'm a dead man. Or at least, someone I care about will die.

I nod as I push past him. It's not like it was my fault I didn't get married last time. Rialta was the one who passed out, not me. And I didn't have anything to do with poisoning her.

Lennox has an empty seat next to him, with Gage and Hayes sitting directly behind him. Rialta and River sit together, so I leave my bag with one of the attendants and slump into the chair next to Lennox, happy to not have to play the doting fiancé for a few hours.

"Do you know what you're doing?" Lennox leans over and asks me.

"Not a clue."

I tilt my head back and close my eyes, knowing I'm not going to figure it out here with everyone watching us so closely. It's looking more and more like I'm going to marry Rialta. I'm going to break River's heart. I'm going to convince the guys to take her as far away as possible. That's the only way to keep her safe.

The flight is mostly uneventful. Everyone sticks to their groups—Corsi with his men, me with mine, and the girls at the back.

When we land, Corsi and his men disappear without a word. "That was strange," Lennox whispers.

I nod. *What is Corsi up to?*

I don't know why he would agree to fly us all to Vegas when we could have just as easily gotten married in Chicago. Maybe his daughter has him wrapped around her finger more than I thought.

When we walk off the plane, a large SUV and a driver are waiting to take us to our hotel. The guys and I climb in the back first while we wait for the attendants to load our luggage and the girls to get on.

"What are you guys doing here?" I ask.

"We figured you would need us for whatever the plan is," Hayes says, patting my shoulder from the row behind me.

"I needed you to protect my family," I say.

"They're safe," Lennox says.

"How do you know that if you aren't with them?"

"We have them on surveillance. They're safe. Corsi has some of his best men protecting them," Gage says.

"You mean holding them hostage," I growl.

The guys are silent until Gage pipes up a moment later. "Corsi will keep his word; you know that. And the second you marry Rialta, you'll have power. You will be able to have some pull with the men. Corsi won't threaten that by hurting them in any way."

"I know, but…"

"But what if you don't marry Rialta?" Lennox asks.

I don't answer. I can't consider that option—it would ruin too many lives. I have to marry her.

Lennox looks to the other two, and they all hold their tongues. No one has any answers for me.

River and Rialta climb into the SUV. River doesn't make eye contact with any of them, but Rialta turns around in the front seat and looks at all of us.

"I'm Rialta Corsi. I don't think we've ever been formally introduced."

"I'm Lennox."

"Gage."

"Hayes."

She waves cutely at them all. "Are we ready for one hell of a wedding weekend?"

None of the guys respond.

She laughs. "Don't worry; I'll get you guys excited soon enough."

"That sounds ominous," Lennox leans over and says.

"You have no idea," I say back.

Rialta insists that the radio be turned on full blast as we drive to our hotel on the strip. She dances around in her seat and even gets River to smile and go along with her at one point. I can't keep my eyes off River—especially when she smiles. All I want is to see her smile, to see her genuinely happy.

Upon arriving at the hotel, I realize I have no idea what the room breakdown is going to be or what tonight or tomorrow holds. The night is still early; the sun has just set. How many hours do I have left before I'm a married man again?

I'm pretty sure I hate the idea of marriage at this point. I'd be happy to never get married again.

River's eye catches mine as she climbs out of the car, and I know it's not true—I'd marry her in a heartbeat. I'd marry her day after day after day if that's what she wanted.

I turn to the guys before I get out. "Be ready for anything."

Hayes snickers. "You are so going to get us all killed, aren't you?"

"I honestly don't know what I'm going to do."

"You've got it so bad, dude," Lennox laughs. "I hope when the rest of us find love, it doesn't start a war along with it."

I sigh.

"I don't want to think about any of you falling in love right now. We can only take one lovesick idiot at a time," Gage says.

We head into the flashy hotel full of people, and we all go into protective mode. In a busy crowd like this, it would be easy for anyone to hurt or kidnap Rialta. I have no idea why Corsi agreed to this unless he thinks our enemies are far behind us, possibly still in Chicago.

Rialta holds up a key, running over to us. "Daddy sprung for the penthouse suite. Come on, everyone! You're crashing in our room tonight."

I raise my eyebrows as she throws herself in my embrace.

"Are you sure about that? Don't you want to have a nice, peaceful, quiet night alone?" I ask. It doesn't surprise me that Corsi sprung for the most expensive room in this place, but I'm not sure I can handle being so close to River.

"Nope, tonight is about celebrating, having fun, and getting drunk. Let's party, people!" Rialta yells.

Hayes chuckles. "And I thought I was the most obnoxious one. Seems like I've been outdone."

I turn and look at the guys as I walk Rialta to the elevators while the others follow. I give them a look of desperation, but they just chuckle and shrug.

I sigh as I step onto the elevator with Rialta. She holds the door until everyone else gets on.

Hayes wraps his arm casually over River's shoulder as she steps on and whispers something into her ear that earns him a genuine smile.

Fuck, I have to stop staring at her.

I turn my attention to Rialta. "So the plan for tonight is to get drunk in the room?"

"Yep!" She almost jumps up and down at the thought.

"Happen to know where your father is?"

She shrugs. "Setting up surveillance on this place, I'm sure."

I nod.

"Stop pouting; this is supposed to be a fun night. You only get married once, and this is your last night of freedom," she says.

I cock my head. "Actually—"

She laughs. "Oops, I guess it's not your first rodeo. But it's mine, so let's have some fun for once and stop thinking about all the people who want us dead."

Suddenly, she plants a kiss on my lips. I gasp as she does because I'm not ready. I'm never ready for her kisses. And I'm definitely not prepared when my lips part, and she shoves tongue halfway down my throat. Or when her soft moan vibrates through my mouth. Or when her hand grabs onto my ass and squeezes.

She's definitely gotten more brazen since that first timid kiss.

A throat clears, and we stop kissing.

"Come on, you two lovebirds, don't keep hogging the elevators," Hayes says with River still under his arm as he keeps the elevator door open for us.

Rialta grabs my hand and drags me off.

I force myself not to look at River. The best plan is still my original plan. By the end of our time here, River should hate me. She should despise me. She should want to throw me over the balcony of this hotel. If I can do that, then we can both move on.

Rialta pulls me through the double doors to our penthouse suite. Instantly, I can see why she wants to share it with everyone—it's huge. I can't even see the end of the hallway from where we stand. Door after door lines one side, which I assume lead to bedrooms and bathrooms. The other side of the hallway opens to spacious, expensive-looking rooms.

Rialta heads in the direction of the bar.

"Make me something, fiancé," Rialta demands.

I'm not sure it's a great idea considering the meds she's been on lately, but there will be no arguing with her tonight. I've never seen her drink. I have no idea how she'll be or how high of a tolerance she has, but I'm guessing she should start with something easy.

I walk behind the bar while she pulls up a seat. She

motions for the others to sit at the other barstools while I play bartender.

I pull out a bottle of champagne to start. It's too sweet for my tastes and probably most of the guys's, but they'll tolerate it if I don't offer anything else. They'll also realize it's so Rialta isn't encouraged to drink harder stuff too early in the night.

I pull out six champagne glasses and start pouring the bottle into them.

"My lady," I say, handing Rialta the first glass of champagne as I bow.

She laughs and takes the drink.

I start passing the rest out to the others, but when I get to River she shakes her head.

"No, thanks," River says.

Rialta frowns. "You have to drink; it's our joint bachelor and bachelorette party."

"Someone should be sober in case we're attacked," River says.

"Nope, that's Dad's job. Tonight, we're all drinking."

I set the glass down in front of River, letting her decide if she wants to deal with disappointing Rialta or not. I'm not going to deal with Rialta's wrath for not handing River her drink.

I take my own glass, and then Rialta lifts her glass up. "To happily ever afters."

"To happily ever afters," everyone says, clinking our glasses together and taking sips. Well, everyone takes a sip except River. She pretends to drink but doesn't actually drink anything. Rialta doesn't notice, but I wish River would drink—it would make the sting hurt less.

Rialta downs her champagne and then runs up to me, dragging me out from behind the bar.

"Someone turn on some music!" she shouts.

"On it," Gage says, getting up. A few seconds later, music is playing throughout the suite.

There is a large outdoor balcony that extends around the entire suite. She pulls me out there where the music can still be heard.

"Dance with me," she commands.

I yank her close against my body, knowing I should lean into this. She has the right attitude—have some fun with this and forget everything else. Forget all the pain and heartbreak. Remember the good that our marriage will do. Try to enjoy each other.

I'm going to need more alcohol.

Hayes pulls River out, and the two of them start dancing next to us.

Don't look at her. Don't look at her. Don't look at her.

I repeat my mantra while I dance with Rialta, but it's impossible to keep up when Lennox and Gage join in, dancing around River like she's the center of their universe. I know they're just trying to distract her and cheer her up as she watches me and Rialta dance, but it still burns just the same.

Rialta looks up at me with heavy eyes. "Kiss me like you love me."

"Rialta, I—"

"I know you don't, and that's okay. I'm not asking you to love me. I'm asking you to kiss me like you do."

I frown, and my grip on her hip slackens.

"Please," she whispers in such a sincere voice.

I don't know why she wants it. Maybe she wants to know what our future could hold someday if I did ever fall in love with her. Maybe she's not as excited about this marriage as I think. Maybe this is just as hard for her, but how she handles it is by partying and getting drunk.

I can give her this. I can try, at least.

I yank her tight to my body until we are pressed as close together as we can be. My hand slips down to her ass, squeezing tightly, and then I dip her back just a little as my lips come down hungrily against hers, devouring her.

My eyes are closed tight as my tongue sweeps across hers, and a demanding growl leaves my throat, claiming her. I let my hand run up her body, twisting her hair in a fist and yanking her back as my teeth come down on her bottom lip.

She whimpers against me as her eyes flutter open and her cheeks flush.

"Was that enough for you?" I ask.

Her eyes cut away for a second and then back to me. "That was perfect."

I smirk, knowing she's all hot and bothered because of that kiss. Her face is flushed, and she runs her tongue across her lip. She takes a deep breath and then says, "Are you ready?"

I blink, not understanding what she means. "Ready for what?"

"Ready to get married tonight?"

My heart skips a beat, my breath catches in my throat, and a knot forms in my stomach. I don't want to get married to her. I don't want to get married to her ever. But it might be best to rip the bandaid off before I do something stupid that will get someone I love killed.

"I thought you wanted to get married tomorrow? You don't have a dress. I don't have a tux. We don't have rings or—"

She puts a finger over my lips, shutting me up.

"We need to do it spontaneously. There is less of a chance of someone interrupting it, of things getting ruined."

I know she's right, but the dread in my stomach is overwhelming. I'm never going to feel right ever again. I'm never going to know real love. I'm always going to be separated from the one I love.

But River will be alive. She'll be safe. And she'll have a chance at happiness someday.

"Okay," I say.

I'm going to need a stronger drink to get me down the aisle.

15
RI

I'VE NEVER SEEN someone find a chapel so fast. Or rush half a dozen people out of a hotel suite that fast. I don't know what the rush is or if she arranged this all with Vincent without me, but the transition was whiplashing. Within minutes we go from dancing on the roof, drinking champagne, and trying to keep my eyes anywhere but on Rialta and Beckett making out to jumping into a waiting limo.

Yea, Rialta definitely planned this.

She's all over Beckett in the limo as Hayes starts pouring everyone more champagne.

"Wait! No one can drink anything else!" Rialta says.

Hayes stops mid-pour. "Why not?"

"Last time I drank something before my wedding, I got poisoned."

Hayes looks at the bottle and then sighs, putting it back down. "I don't know how we are supposed to get through tonight on one glass of champagne," he mumbles to me.

I smile tightly. "Once we get to the chapel, I'm getting

drunk. I don't care what she says. I tried it sober, and it damn near killed me. You guys are going to need to be on your best behavior to keep everyone safe."

Hayes grumbles some more but agrees and passes on the message to the other two, who nod at me. They've got my back; they always do.

The limo stops outside of a chapel, and I feel like vomiting. How can this be happening so quickly? Last time I was prepared. I hadn't seen them together yet. I told myself it was for the best. But now, actually seeing them together, it feels like I'm about to attend my own funeral, not a wedding.

The second Rialta is out, I lean over to Hayes. "Hand me that bottle."

He happily hands it to me, and I gulp down several swigs before getting out of the limo. The second I'm outside and I see her holding his hand and kissing him again, I realize no amount of alcohol is going to help. I feel stone-cold sober.

"Fuck," I curse.

Hayes, Lennox, and Gage surround me, putting their arms on or around me.

"Don't lose faith. Even if they get married, it doesn't mean that's the end for you and him," Lennox says.

I nod, but he's wrong. If Beckett marries her, that will be it. There will be no going back. The mafia won't allow it.

We head into the chapel, where Rialta is talking giddily to the receptionist.

"We have thirty minutes until our time slot. Guys, head into that room and find something to put on. River, come with me," Rialta says, skipping into a room that says, 'For Brides.'

Hayes smiles at me encouragingly. Lennox matches my expression, looking like he's about to be sick. And Gage pulls up his phone, letting me know he's got the security part covered.

I can't look at Beckett. I'm not sure if I'll ever be able to look at him again. I just walk into the room that Rialta just disappeared into.

"Wow," I say when I see a heaping cart of wedding dresses in the corner.

"The receptionist said we can rent any of the dresses for the wedding. Help me pick one out," Rialta orders.

I walk over to the cart and start combing through them. They are very much what one would expect a chapel in Vegas to have. A lot of very short, skimpy dresses. A couple of boring A-line styles with no shape, so they'll fit practically anyone. And then a couple of big, poofy princess dresses. I hold up a couple of those out to show her.

"These are perfect!" Rialta squeals. She looks them both over and picks the one most likely to fit.

"What about you?" she asks as she starts removing her shirt.

"What about me? There aren't any bridesmaid dresses, and this isn't a typical wedding anyway. It's just about the two of you."

Rialta frowns. "No, you have to wear a dress. I'm over your all-black outfits like you're in mourning or something."

I am in mourning, I think, but can't say out loud.

Rialta walks back over to the cart and starts going through the dresses again.

I sigh and look around, walking over to the veils hoping to find something that will match Rialta's dress.

There is no way she's going to share the spotlight with me, and those dresses are starch white. She should be the only one wearing white today.

"Found it!" Rialta carries a dress over to me.

I turn toward her and freeze.

"It's—" I'm speechless. It's perfect.

"It's perfect for you," Rialta says.

I smile and take the dress. It's a strapless ballgown with a black lace overlay on the bodice and a tulle skirt.

"Are you sure? It still has a lot of white, and I don't want to take away any attention on your wedding day."

"I'm positive. It's perfect for you. Please wear it."

I nod.

She grins, and we both get changed into our dresses. I comb my hand through my hair, and Rialta does the same, resulting in similar long waves.

I wish I would have thought to put a little makeup on.

"Makeup!" Rialta says, holding up her purse.

"You really did think of everything," I laugh.

"I did," she says coyly.

She sits in the makeup chair in front of the mirror and starts applying her makeup.

"So, how long have you had this planned?" I ask.

She shrugs. "A girl has to have some mysteries."

I shake my head. "If you want me to protect you, you really should let me in on what you're thinking sometimes."

"Maybe I don't want you to protect me anymore," she says.

I frown. "What do you mean?"

The door opens suddenly, and Vincent is standing there dumbfounded. I guess he didn't know about this.

"Really, River? You let her plan a wedding and didn't

tell me or my men? How am I supposed to protect—wait, why are you wearing a wedding dress, River?"

"It's a decoy. If someone is trying to attack me, they won't know which of us to attack," Rialta answers before I can open my mouth.

"Good thinking," Vincent takes a step forward.

He walks over to Rialta. "You really do look beautiful."

"Thank you," she beams.

"You both do," he says to me.

I raise my eyebrows, shocked that he gave me a compliment. He almost never does.

"Are you almost ready?" he asks Rialta.

"Almost, but I don't want you or your men in the chapel," Rialta says.

"Why not?"

"Well, for one, that didn't work last time. And two, the chapel is tiny, and we don't want to draw any attention. You're better guards if you are outside, keeping an eye out for intruders," Rialta says.

Vincent frowns.

"Plus, you'll cry, and everyone will know you aren't the tough mafia leader everyone thinks you are. You can't ruin your reputation now," Rialta says.

"Fine, you're probably right. I'm just happy for you, Rialta. I've been planning this for a long time. I wasn't sure we'd ever make it this far. I wasn't sure if I could keep you alive long enough to get married. Your life is still going to be hard going forward, but we will do everything we can to protect you." Vincent pulls her into a hug.

"I know you will." Rialta looks directly at me with defiance. Rialta releases him. "Now get out of here; we have to finish getting ready."

Vincent leaves, and then Rialta turns to me. "Your turn. Let's get some makeup on your pretty face."

I sit in the makeup seat while she applies some eye shadow.

"What did you mean before when you said you don't want me to protect you anymore? Are you rethinking your plan of just having me as your main protection outside of Beckett? I'm sure his guys—Gage, Hayes, and Lennox—would be happy to help protect you. You can trust the three of them as much as you can trust me and Beckett. Or—"

"I don't want to talk about it right now. I just want to think about the wedding. Afterward, we'll talk. I'm sure of it."

She applies some lipstick and blush and then steps back. "Beautiful."

I turn to look at myself in the mirror, studying my dark eyeshadow and red lips. I love how I look. I don't know how she came through with the dresses and makeup, but she did.

We each find some heels in a pile in the corner. Neither of them fit very well, but no one will be looking at our feet.

"Veil?" I ask her, holding up two I think will work with her dress.

She looks between the two of them just as there is a knock at the door.

"It's time," Hayes says, poking his head in.

Rialta snatches a veil from my hand. "Let's go."

Suddenly my stomach is in knots, and huge butterflies are swarming again. This is my last chance to tell her how I feel about Beckett. My last chance to tell him how I feel. My last chance to stop this wedding.

Rialta heads to the door and then realizes I haven't moved. "You coming?"

I nod and follow her.

Hayes is still waiting at the door.

"Tell the guys to head in, and we'll be right there," Rialta says.

Hayes nods and then leaves.

Rialta pokes her head out the door a second. We wait a moment, and then she says, "Come on."

I can see some of Vincent's men standing guard outside the chapel door as Rialta hurries us across the lobby to the doors of the chapel.

"You ready for this?" I ask, plastering an overt smile on my face. I can be happy for her. I can.

She smirks. "Definitely. The question is, are you?"

She throws the veil on my head.

I frown. "What are you doing?"

"Protecting you for once."

She throws the doors open before I realize what's happening.

16

BECKETT

My legs tremble as I stand at the end of the aisle, even though it's a little different this time compared to last. For one, the aisle is about ten feet long, and I don't have the end of a sniper gun aimed at me. This time I don't really need the physical dot on my chest to keep me standing here, not after Corsi came to the groom's room and once again threatened River's life if I don't marry his daughter.

But I can't help my uncontrollable nerves as the wedding march comes over the sound system. I glance over to Lennox, Gage, and Hayes, who are all standing by my side once again. They all nod at me reassuringly. I'm doing the right thing—the only thing I can do to save River right now.

The doors at the back of the chapel open, and I take a deep breath, preparing myself for whatever dress Rialta will be wearing. She steps forward first, and the ballgown she's wearing is as big and fluffy as the one from our first wedding. This one probably cost about a tenth of the other dress and is at least one size too big, but somehow she pulls it off.

I force a smile onto my lips as she walks toward me, but damn, is my smile fake, just like everything about my life is about to be.

Rialta gets to the end, and I hold my arm out to her, preparing myself for what comes next.

"You didn't drink any poisoned wine this time, did you?" I joke. Although, a part of me wishes she did so we could delay this once again. I'm not ready. I'll never be ready.

"Of course not. But the question is, are you ready to finally get your happily ever after?"

My teeth rake over my bottom lip, unsure of how to answer. I don't want to hurt her feelings, not today, but I can't tell her that marrying her is how I get my happily ever after.

Rialta winks at me.

I narrow my eyes, puzzled as she doesn't take my arm. Instead, she steps to the side, mirroring the position of my men on her side of the aisle.

I stare at Rialta, who just motions with her head for me to turn and face the aisle once again. My heart skips several beats because I hope—damn do I hope—when I shouldn't. But I can't stop myself from wishing.

I turn, and the strongest, fiercest, bravest, most beautiful, incredible woman in the entire world is walking toward me. The dress fits her like it was handmade for her —a mix of black and white lace covers the bodice until the dress flares out with tulle at the bottom. Her raven-colored hair is long and wavy, covering her bare shoulders with a veil tucked in the back, her red lipstick popping against the shades of white and black.

She's my dream, my perfect match, and the woman who will push me to be the best version of myself just to keep up with her. But she's walking far too slow for my taste. I need to be married to this woman now.

I run to meet her, holding my arm out to her.

She stares at it like she can't believe it. "I—I don't understand."

I don't have words. I'm still in shock myself, but I know she needs to hear them.

"Rialta isn't the woman for me. She knows that. She saw how in love we are, and she refuses to be a wedge between us. You've protected her for almost your entire life; now it's her turn to protect you."

"I know, and I'm grateful, but I can't—Vincent will kill you." She tries to pull away, but I link my fingers through hers, stopping her.

I grin widely. "I never promised I'd marry Rialta."

"What? Of course, you did."

"No, I promised I'd marry his daughter. And you are as much his daughter as Rialta is."

Her lips part, but she doesn't say anything. She won't argue with me, which tells me she wants this as much as I do.

I closely stand in front of her to narrow her field of vision to just me. I grip her hand and stare deeply into her eyes.

"Do you love me?" I ask.

She swallows hard against the lump in her throat. "Yes, I love you. I've always loved you. I never stopped loving you."

"Same. I love you, River. I've always loved you, even when I shouldn't. And I never stopped loving you even when you tried to push me away."

She bites her bottom lip.

"Do you want to marry me?" I ask.

Her eyes drop, and look away.

"River Corsi, do you want to marry me? Don't think of anything else. Don't think about the consequences or the fear or anything; just answer the question. Do you want to marry me?"

Her chest rises and falls deeply, and then her face lifts, and she looks at me with a smirk. "You call that a proposal? I'm pretty sure you can do better than that," she teases.

I laugh, wrapping my arm around her tightly and spinning her around.

She laughs too before I set her feet back on the ground. "I'll marry you," she says in a whisper against my ear.

"Then let's go get married," I say with a now permanent grin.

With our fingers intertwined, we walk the rest of the short distance down the aisle. The wedding march is still playing, and it stops playing the second we reach the end of the aisle.

"I'm scared," River whispers next to me.

"You face a room full of dangerous men without breaking a sweat, but getting married to me is what makes you scared?" I tease, trying to calm her nerves, but I'm just as terrified.

I'm not afraid of marrying her—it's not a mistake, unlike my previous weddings. No, I'm terrified that I'm dreaming—I'll wake up, and this won't be real, or someone will try and take her away from me.

Her eyes are big as she looks at me. "I'm terrified of losing you, but this—this isn't a mistake. This is the best decision either of us has ever made."

A woman steps forward in a tux and starts the ceremony. I barely look at the officiant, just enough to know where we are in the ceremony; mostly I just stare at River.

"Would you like to say traditional vows or your own?" the officiant asks.

"Our own," both River and I say at the same time.

"Ladies first," I say.

River faces me, gripping my hand with both of hers, doing anything to prevent this from disappearing.

"I, River Corsi, have nothing. I'm no mafia princess. I have no inheritance. No title, no empire or kingdom. I have very little money and very few skills outside of being a good shot."

"With a great right hook," Hayes jokes.

River smiles. "What I do have are a lot of enemies. I have a father who will want to kill us both for this. A future with me is bleak. But I can offer you one thing, Beckett—I promise that I will never stop loving you.

"I loved you when I found out you were married. I loved you when you lied to me. When you tried to break me. When you pretended to love another woman. I loved you despite all the heartache. You're the other piece of me. I love you when we fight and bicker. I love you when you're being sweet and romantic. But most of all, I love you for saving me from myself. I love you, Hero."

I blink, and a tear rolls down my cheek. I didn't realize how much of a romantic I am until I met her.

"I, Beckett, am a monster. I've done horrible things. I've stolen, beaten, and killed. I've risked the lives of my family and friends. I'm no prince. While I have plenty of money, I have no kingdom. No title, no group that I belong to—not anymore. I have little more to offer you than being skilled with a gun, although my right hook is nowhere near as good as yours."

She blushes and laughs at that.

"But I can offer you my love—all of my heart. It's always belonged to you. I've fought it so many times. I've tried to stop loving you—it would have been easier for everyone if I had succeeded, but there is no way for me to stop loving you, ever. You're a drug to me, and I'm addicted to you.

"You think you have nothing to offer—no title, no money, no kingdom, but you're everything to me. You make me a better person. To me, you're my queen. And you've saved me more times than I can count. I could vow all the normal things—to be loyal and faithful and honest with you until death do us part, but I'm not going to. In our world, we do what we must to survive. I'll only make one vow—the same vow you made to me. I promise I'll love you forever, Queen."

We stare at each other without blinking, without breathing. I'm pretty sure our hearts have stopped, likely so we can rip them out and give them to the other.

"Do you have rings you'd like to exchange?" the officiant asks us.

"No—" I start to reply.

"Yes," Rialta and Lennox say at the same time.

My eyes shift from Rialta to Lennox, completely confused with how they both have rings. Were these rings made for me and Rialta? Or did they plan this switcheroo?"

I take the ring from Lennox, and River takes the ring from Rialta. We each hold them in front of us to look at them. It's clear that Rialta, and it seems Lennox, each got rings for the two of us. The rings each have words etched into them.

River's smile lights up the room as she takes my hand

and pushes the ring onto my finger, reading the etching as she does.

"I'll love you forever, Hero."

I can barely contain myself as the ring slides onto my finger.

I take her ring, which is thinner but otherwise as black and plain as mine. She's not really a diamonds girl anyway. It's exactly what I would have picked for her. I take her hand and slide the ring onto her finger.

"I promise forever, Queen."

Her eyes widen when I say 'queen,' and she looks down to see those words etched into the ring.

"How?" she looks from me to Lennox.

"We figured 'princess' was our word for you, and Beckett has always thought of you as more, so we took a wild guess with Queen." Lennox pats my shoulder. "But it was a stroke of genius on our parts since he included it in his vows."

"Lucky guess, not genius," I say, pushing Lennox back.

I look to the officiant, in desperate need of the next part, because I'm dying to kiss her.

The officiant smiles knowingly. "You are officially married. I can now pronounce you husband and wife. You may kiss your bride."

Before she finishes, my lips are on River's, and someone is going to have to pry me away to get me to stop.

17
RI

It's all a dream—it has to be. Any minute now, I'm going to wake up and realize this too is just a figment of my imagination, just like every dirty dream I've had about him these last few days.

But when he presses his lips against mine, reality hits me full force. His kiss is better than anything I've been dreaming about.

I fall into the kiss, and everything else drifts away. All the fear, the worry, the danger, everyone else—it all vanishes.

My entire world is the two of us kissing.

His lips feel like heaven against mine, and when he dips his tongue into my mouth, it's with a promise of walking through hell for me. I'm not a passive participant in the kiss either. My tongue battles his back.

I don't know what our future holds or if our marriage is to only last days, maybe even hours, before our lives are threatened. But what I do know, as his tongue whips through my mouth, is that we are in this together. We are putting each other first.

We are done pretending that we don't love each other. We are done pretending we are okay being with other people to protect each other. We will protect what we have together.

"Alright, you two lovebirds. We need to get out of here before Father figures out what happened," Rialta says.

Beckett and I break our kiss, revealing goofy grins on our faces. Neither of us is going to be able to stop smiling. I don't care if a hundred men enter the room with guns right now it won't wipe the smiles from our faces or get us to stop staring at each other.

"The limo is waiting in the back; let's go," Rialta says. She motions past us to the guys, knowing she's going to need their help to get us to do anything.

Lennox starts pushing Beckett from behind as Rialta pulls on my arm, and we walk through the back of the chapel. As we get to the back door, Rialta turns and looks at me.

"I need to borrow this." She snatches my veil from atop my head and puts it on her own. "And I need to borrow your husband for just a second."

I glare at her with a deep frown.

Everyone laughs, but I don't find it particularly funny.

Rialta rolls her eyes. "I'll give him right back, I promise."

She hooks her arm through Beckett's, yanking him forward before he can protest. The second we step outside, I see why she stole my veil and husband—some of Vincent's men are back here waiting for us.

She smiles and waves at them as she drags Beckett into the limo. The rest of us quickly climb in.

"We're ready to go," Rialta says to the driver through

an intercom system, and we're off. She turns to me. "You can have him back now."

She motions for us to switch seats, and I quickly climb to the back next to Beckett. She takes a spot between Lennox and Hayes.

Beckett wastes no time, grabbing my neck and turning me toward him to get another kiss in. I get lost in the kiss —memorizing every touch of his hand, press of his lips, lap of his tongue, and scrape of his teeth. It's automatic after everything we've been through. Every time we've kissed or fucked, it felt like a goodbye. For once, this feels like the first of many.

"To Mr. and Mrs. Beckett and River Corsi," Rialta hoops and hollers at us.

We stop kissing, but we can't stop smiling.

"Corsi, huh? You going to take my last name?" I ask.

"Beckett was technically my last name. My first name is Eli, but everyone calls me Beckett. When I married Odette, they changed my first name to Beckett and made me take her last name of Monroe. I don't care what my name is; I just want it to be tied to you. So, Beckett Corsi it is."

I grin. "I like it. River and Beckett Corsi."

We both turn our attention to the others. "I'm going to kill you for putting me through that, Rialta," I say.

She smirks at me. "You got your prince charming, so I'd say it was worth it."

"Why, though? Why not just tell me your plan? Why make out with him constantly and dry hump him in front of me?"

"I had to be sure of your feelings. You would never voluntarily put yourself ahead of me, so I had to play detective. The easiest way to figure out how you felt was to see if I could make you jealous. If I could, then I'd know you loved him."

"And if didn't get jealous? If it didn't appear I loved him?"

Rialta shrugs, drinking a sip of her champagne. "Then I would have married him. He's plenty good-looking, and he's an excellent kisser."

I glare at her, and the entire limo laughs.

"Hey, look at me," Beckett says, turning my attention back to him. "You got me. Don't think about all the times she kissed me; think about what I'm going to do to you when we get to the hotel."

"Why do we have to wait until we get to the hotel?" I breathe against his ear. If this life has taught me anything, it's that if I want something, I should never wait. Anything and everything can be taken from me in a split second, and right now, I want my husband.

Beckett doesn't hesitate either. He pulls me onto his lap as my lips land back on his. I can hear the others conversing, but it's merely background noise. All that matters right now is him. I need him right now.

I grab either side of his jaw as I plant a hot and heavy kiss on him. I can't hold back, and it makes him instantly hard beneath me.

He bucks once against me, letting me feel the full length of him as we kiss. I grind on top of him, needing him so desperately that I'll burst if I don't have him soon.

"Hurry," I whisper against his ear while his hand dives under my dress and rips my panties in half.

I need his touch. I need his cock. I need all of him—all of him that I never thought I'd get again.

He kisses down my neck, sucking hard and not bothering to be gentle while his fingers push between my folds, finding my sensitive clit and stroking it.

"Fuck," I moan against his shoulder at the simple touch. I know we have an audience, and I should be quiet, but I don't care. Everyone in this limo has seen me naked. Everyone has seen me struggle with loving him but not being allowed to have him. I don't care if everyone sees me come on my husband's dick for the first time.

"You're such a naughty, dirty girl, Ri," he whispers in my ear.

I run my tongue over his ear. "I don't care. I want you, and I won't wait another second."

I yank on his pants then, undoing the belt, button, and zipper. His fingers continue to work over my clit until I can barely contain my arousal. It makes it difficult to concentrate on what I'm doing, but I eventually free him from his pants.

I waste no time climbing on top of him. I need him more than I've ever needed anything, and it's clear from the hunger in his eyes that he needs me too.

His hand on my hip helps guide me down at the same time he thrusts up. I gasp as he fills me in a way no other man has—all the way to my heart.

The growl he releases is loud and ferocious. He doesn't hold back. He doesn't care about the others in the limo, so neither do I.

I cry out as I move my hips over his cock. It's a feeling I never thought I'd get to experience again. I can feel literal tears in my eyes as I feel him move inside me.

I grab his neck again and kiss him hard. My forcefulness is going to leave us both bruised and bloodied, but I don't care. I don't care if our teeth clash or one of us bites down on the other too hard. It's just raw passion and hunger driving our kisses.

He pulls me back when my wet tears drip down my cheeks onto his face. He kisses every single one, taking away all of my pain as he continues to thrust inside me.

"This is real. I'm yours, and you're mine," he whispers. His voice cracks, and I can hear his pain. He, too, thought this would never happen again.

"This is real," I pant back as I kiss every inch of his skin I can access. I want his clothes off so I can kiss him fucking everywhere, but I can't fucking stop to strip him.

He drives harder into me, and I can barely hang on as I meet his thrusts, grinding my hips harder over his body.

"I love you," I pant, feeling free to say the words for the first time in a long time.

He grins. "Say it again."

"I love you. I love you. I love you," I chant over and over as my orgasm builds.

And then I'm exploding—my climax erupting through my body. I scream. I cry out. I gasp. I moan and groan. So many sounds leave my body as a lifetime of agony is released as well.

Beckett pumps into me one more time before filling me with his warm cum.

My head falls forward against his, and my eyes close. I don't need him to say anything; I can feel everything he's feeling.

"I love you too, my queen. I love you, Princess. I love you, Ri. I love you, River. I love you, my wife," he pants.

I grin each time he speaks words my heart has been aching to hear. Even if he felt them, I never thought those words would ever be spoken out loud. He had agreed to marry Rialta.

Rialta!

I still as Beckett's cock still rests inside me, the reality of what we just did overcoming me and my cheeks beginning to flush. I try to look out of the corner of my eye to see our friends' reactions, but I can't see without moving my head.

Beckett opens his eyes with a sly smirk on his face.

"What?" I ask.

"I love that you have no problem fucking me in front of others, but the second we're done, you turn redder than an apple. I don't think I've ever seen your cheeks so red," he chuckles.

I take a deep breath. "Well, I've fucked every guy in this limo." I lower my voice. "But it's strange to fuck you in front of Rialta. Twenty minutes ago, she was the one who you were supposed to marry."

Beckett's face darkens. "Would you change anything? Would you take it all back and not be married to me to spare your sister's feelings?"

I look deep into Beckett's eyes. "I wouldn't change anything. I didn't need to be married to you. Marriage is just a legal piece of paper our society has decided means something, but I am thankful for it.

"It means we belong to each other. It makes it harder for others to steal you away from me. You're mine. I would marry you again in a heartbeat, and I wouldn't take back that fuck for anything in the world."

He grins.

"But I'm sorry for Rialta," I say, still facing Beckett.

He laughs.

"What?" I ask.

"Turn around."

I don't know what will be behind me when I turn

around, but what I see shocks me—a completely empty limo.

I turn back around, ready to lay into Beckett.

He's dying with laughter at my reaction. "They left the second you climbed on top of me."

I frown and jab him playfully on the shoulder.

"Fuck," Beckett curses, but it doesn't stop him from laughing, so I hit him a second time.

I climb off of him.

"You should have told me," I scold.

"Why? I wanted to see how much you wanted me. I needed to see it. I almost married Rialta because I didn't think you loved me. That was the only way I could ever agree to marry someone else, by the way. Even if marrying her was the best way to protect you and everyone else I care about, I could never have done it if I wasn't convinced, on some level, that you didn't love me."

"You thought I didn't love you?" I ask.

He shrugs. "I could make arguments for either. I thought several women loved me in the past, and I was always wrong. I don't trust my judgment."

I take his hand and put it against my heart. "And now?"

He smirks. "Now, I'm more sure than ever that I've found a woman who not only loves me but will fuck me in front of an audience to show me her love."

"I hate you," I lie with a grin.

"I hate you, too," he lies back with a gleam in his eye.

"Now what?" I ask.

He looks down at his watch. "Tomorrow, we face reality. We have to figure out a plan on how to face it, but not tonight."

"Are we going back to the suite with everyone? I'm not

sure I'm ready to face them. Tonight, I just want you all to myself," I beg.

"I couldn't agree more," he says mischievously. He's up to something, something I'm probably going to like way too much.

18

BECKETT

Fucking her was heaven. I have no idea how I was able to hold on so long. It was so incredible I thought I was coming to come like a teenager within a minute of fucking her.

Through the intercom, I tell our driver to drop us off at the hotel next to our original hotel. If they need us, they can find us quickly, but I'm hoping we can get some alone time.

I text Lennox to tell Rialta and the others to stay hidden in the suite until morning. We need tonight alone, without anyone knowing we got married. Tomorrow we will face reality. Tomorrow we will figure out what to do about Corsi and everything else.

I turn my phone off. No matter what happens, I don't want to know about it until the morning. I made that clear to Lennox—I'm leaving him in charge, and I'm not to be bothered until morning, no matter what.

Ri and I need tonight. If we are going to figure out how to survive this world, we need tonight.

The limo stops in front of the hotel, and I take Ri's

hand, leading her through the lobby. There's a line at the front desk, but I'll be dammed if I'm going to wait in it. I walk straight up to the front desk.

"I need a room, any room," I say.

"Sir, the line starts—"

The glare I give him shuts him up. I toss my credit card and ID at him impatiently, while River tries to hide her smile at my impatience. She doesn't seem bothered that we just cut half a dozen people in line.

We may be married, and I may have gotten to fuck her already, but that's nowhere near enough to satisfy me. And with our luck, the few hours left in the night might be all we have. I'm not wasting a single second of it.

The man behind the counter grins. "All we have left are our presidential suites."

He probably thinks I can't afford an expensive suite, what with us not booking a hotel room in advance, and my tux and her dress screaming trashy Vegas wedding. But money isn't the problem.

"Great. I'll pay double if you hand me the key in the next five seconds."

The key magically finds its way into my hand, but I think it takes more like ten seconds instead of five. I grab River's hand again, and we race to the elevator. Thankfully, the elevator opens the second she presses the button, and I pull her on.

We're practically panting, but all I allow myself is to hold her hand as the elevator slowly rises to the top floor.

"After all of that, you aren't even going to kiss me?" River asks.

I stare at the numbers as we ascend. "If I do more than this, we'll never leave this elevator. I'll fuck you against the wall. The cops will be called, and we'll spend tonight in jail."

She laughs. "You can't carry me down the hall like in the movies?"

"I have no control when it comes to you."

The doors open, but before I can tug on her hand, she starts running, and I give chase.

"What are you doing?" I shout after her.

"Putting us both out of our misery as fast as possible," she smiles back.

She stops in front of the suite door, and I almost slam into her. I take the key out of my pocket but hesitate a second.

"God, it's good to see your genuine smile. I thought I'd never see it again. I thought I'd get glaring, growling, sulking Ri for the rest of my life," I say.

"Open that door, and you can get moaning, screaming, coming Ri." She wiggles her eyebrows, and I capture her mouth with mine. I purposefully keep the kiss soft and light because I really want to double-check the security of the room before I fuck her. I want one incredible night without worry, and I need a clear brain to check the room.

When I pull back, her eyes are glossy, and her lips are swollen. "I thought you couldn't control yourself around me?"

"I can't."

I push the door open and brush past her, pulling my gun out as I search the room. I see her out of the corner of her eye, pulling a gun out from her outer thigh.

"You were made for me; you know that?" I say.

She rakes her teeth over her bottom lip. "And you were made for me. Now let's do a quick scan and barricade the door."

I nod, and we both go to work searching the multiple bedrooms, bathrooms, and living spaces. The suite is massive and over the top, similar to the penthouse Rialta has in the hotel next door. I want to curse the man behind the front desk for giving us this room, not because of how expensive or extravagant it is, but because of how fucking long it takes us to secure it.

When I make my way back to the front door, River already has it locked up with a chair wedged until the door handle. She really isn't taking any chances of being interrupted.

We're both still gripping our guns when our gazes meet. We've both been through so much, but this moment feels bigger than anything we've ever done. We might be married on paper, but we've lied and betrayed and hurt each other all for the sake of love. There's a lot of healing that needs to happen between the two of us. It starts with opening our chests and baring our hearts to each other, wounds and all.

Ri starts to walk toward me. Her tongue runs across her bottom lip, her eyes dilate with need, and her hands tremble. With each step, I see her knees almost buckle.

My own body mirrors hers—filled with lust and yet terrified.

She stops a foot away from me.

We both take a breath, unsure of where to start. *With words? With making out? With fucking? What will heal us? What will bind us together?*

Ri decides, taking charge before I can make up my mind. She jumps onto me, throwing her legs and arms around my body and crashing her lips down on mine.

Her lips on mine feel like the best place to start. That is

until I feel her kick my gun out of my hand and aim hers at my heart.

"No more lies. No more betrayals. No more hiding things from me in the name of trying to save me. You said you'd never be my hero."

"And yet, you call me Hero," I say.

I eye the gun aimed at my chest. It's meant to threaten me, to make me vulnerable. She doesn't need the gun to do that, and I know she won't shoot me. It's just how we work.

"I call you Hero because that's what you are. It's why we've gotten into this mess. It's why you keep staying married to or almost marrying other people. I'm more than capable of taking care of myself."

I snatch the gun out of her hand and slam her back into the wall. "Are you?"

She narrows her eyes and bares her teeth at me. "You know I am."

I drop the gun and grab her jaw to kiss her hard, taking her breath away.

She melts against me and then does exactly what I would expect from her—she kicks me in the balls to free herself and send me crumpling to the ground. She stands over me, her legs on either side of my head, and the view makes me forget about the bruising pain in my balls.

I wrap my hand around her ankle and yank hard, forcing her to her knees on top of me. Her pussy lands on my face, and I lick up the length of her. Her legs shiver over me. I hold her tight, getting a better taste of her. She's already wet, her lips swollen for me, ready for me to take her, and we've barely even started.

But we need this. We need this fight to get our emotions out. We need a fresh start.

She doesn't let me lick her for long, even though she loves what I do to her body. She needs answers, just like I do.

She reaches for something nearby. I don't see what it is until I feel sharp glass at my throat as she straddles me.

"No more playing the hero role," she demands.

I shake my head. "I can't promise that any more than you can."

She growls. "I don't need you to save me. Promise me, or this is over. We are over. I need to be your partner, not your damsel in distress."

I grab her arm and roll us over until I'm straddling her and the piece of glass is pushed against her neck. "Promise me you will never risk your life to protect mine."

Her lips part, but no words come out. She can't do it either.

We should give up right here and now. This is the one promise neither of us can give. And it's the one promise we both need for this relationship to work. It's not worth risking everything our marriage will cause if we can't figure this out.

She sees the defeat in my eyes, but she's far more stubborn than I am. Thank god for her.

She shoves me off of her. I scramble to my feet quickly, expecting another assault. She won't stop attacking until I've made the vow she needs to hear. And if I don't, we'll be locked in this circle of lust and pain and desire forever.

She runs at me and grabs a chandelier at the last second, lifting herself up and wrapping her legs around my head. Her thighs become a vice grip around my head that could easily suffocate me, but all I can think about is tasting her again if I can lift her dress up.

I stumble back against a wall, a picture frame digging

into my back. I jerk forward enough for it to fall to the floor. With my teeth, I grab onto the hem of her dress, and with my hand, I rip straight up. The material is cheap and thin, so I'm able to rip her dress all the way up in two.

River tightens her thighs around my head.

"Please," she says.

I don't know if her word is a cry for my vow or for my tongue on her wetness. I go with option two.

I bury my face between her legs. She squeezes her legs fiercely, but the second my tongue licks up her slit, she melts a little. Her thighs unclench and her hands grip my head, keeping me in place.

"Fuck, you taste delicious," I moan.

"Don't stop."

It's a trap. Everything is always a trap with her, but I don't care. I feast on her.

She grabs for my tie as I feel her close to coming.

I grin against her lips as my tongue dips inside her sweetness.

She gasps, unprepared for the orgasm I've just demanded from her. Then she's screaming my name.

I can't keep my balance, and I stumble away from the wall. She has no control either but holds onto my tie, pulling it so hard I can't breathe.

I stumble through the hotel room with her atop me, grabbing for walls and ending up knocking more decor to the floor. She hangs onto me for dear life.

I fall—we're going down hard. I don't know where we're landing, but I suspect it's going to fucking hurt. Instead, I'm met with the softness of a bed.

Thank fuck.

I roll on top of her, pinning her hands over her head.

"We can't make these demands of each other. We can't, baby."

She struggles against my hold, hating to be constrained. I'm strong enough to hold her with one hand, but I'm not naive enough to think she isn't capable of getting out of my hold.

"Don't call me baby."

I smirk. "That's what you have a problem with? You don't want me to let you go?"

She rolls her eyes. "Why would I care about that when I can do this?" In an instant, she has me facedown with my arm pulled behind my back.

"Have I told you how much I love you lately, *baby*?" I chuckle.

Her teeth are at my ear, about to bite it off as she pulls my arm further, nearly popping it out of my shoulder.

"That's not my name," she growls.

"You can understand why I'd be confused about what to call you. Princess? Ri? Rialta? River? Fighter? Queen? What should I call you?"

She growls.

I laugh as she starts removing my clothes, ripping them from my body piece by piece. I don't fight it. I'm ready to get this tux off and feel her on my skin.

The second all of my clothes are off, I flip over, and she's straddling me.

I expect to see the fierce fighter in her eyes, but I'm confused by the pure agony present as well.

I narrow my eyes as I try to figure out what she's looking at. I follow her gaze and find that she's staring at my tattoo—the one Rialta inked herself.

She jumps off of me and heads to the bathroom.

"Ri!" I chase her, but the bathroom door slams in my face. My fist slams against it.

"Ri, open the door."

She doesn't.

"It's not what it looks like, just—" I try again.

I sigh and start picking the lock on the door, knowing she's not going to let me in.

When I finally get the door open, she's simply standing there, facing the mirror, completely naked.

I want to scoop her up in my arm, but that's not what she wants. She needs to deal with this—the feelings that I was about to marry another woman. She watched Odette and me together, I've caused her immense pain, and there is very little I can do except apologize for my part.

I can't take away the pain. I just hope that being with me is worth the heartbreak she felt before. She wasn't alone in feeling tortured; I felt it too.

But no more.

"I'm sorry," I say, barely over a whisper. That seems like the place to start.

"I'm sorry for marrying Odette. I'm sorry for agreeing to marry Rialta. I'm sorry for protecting you and hurting you. I'm sorry."

She doesn't look at me, but her shoulders slump a little, and her breathing slows. She heard me and accepts my apology.

"On the bed," she says in an annoyingly calm voice.

I take a deep breath but don't argue. I walk to the bed and lie down, waiting for her—to extract more revenge, to fuck, to forgive me? I don't know, but she can take whatever she needs from my body.

A second later, she's hovering over me with a lit candle she must have found in the bathroom.

I look at her suspiciously. "What's that for?"

"For burning that tattoo off your skin," she says slowly.

She tilts the candle, and hot wax drips onto my chest.

"And if this won't work, I'll cut it off," she says, her voice dripping in heartbreak.

She tilts the candle again, but I grab her wrist before it drips. For one, the candle definitely won't burn the tattoo off. For two, she needs to face it.

"Stop."

"No." Tears race down her cheeks.

"Look at the tattoo."

She looks away.

"Look at it, goddammit!" I yell.

She still doesn't.

"Please, for me. Please," I say as soothingly as I can. I need to control myself around her.

I take her hand and place it over my tattoo. Then I wait and wait and wait.

More tears stream before she finally decides to look.

I carefully trace her hand over the tattoos. We trace over the original tattoo the Retribution Kings gave me and then over the new crown—the one Rialta did.

"There's a reason the guys wrote 'queen' on your ring. They knew I thought of you as my queen. They knew this tattoo Rialta gave me was for you, not her. Look."

I trace her fingers over the word 'Ri.'

She stares at it intently as I try to explain.

"Rialta wrote 'Ri.' Even then, she knew there was a chance I wouldn't marry her. She gave me a choice. I chose you as much as you chose me. It's always been you."

"No," River says.

"No?"

She sobs and tilts her head down, her hair covering her face.

"No, she knew who you'd choose; that's why she wrote Ri. She hates nicknames like that. No one ever calls her Ri. That's my name, not hers."

She lifts her head, revealing dried eyes and a beautiful smile.

I exhale a deep breath and wrap my arm around her, pulling her into my chest.

"I love you so much. I'm so sorry, so sorry for all the pain I've caused you," I say.

Her lips fall on mine, kissing me like she's never kissed me before. I can taste her salty, painful tears but also her intense hope in the kiss.

Neither of us has had hope in a long time. We've been too focused on the reality of our situation. But now, we can have hope again.

"I need you. We still have a lot to figure out. A lot of pain to work through. A lot of promises about the future, but I need you—now," she says.

I grin and slide her hips down until my cock is straining at her entrance. I ease her down onto me, our lips and eyes never leaving each other.

"We really have a fucked up sense of foreplay, don't we?" I whisper.

She laughs. "I like our foreplay." Her eyes twinkle.

"Oh yeah?"

"Yeah."

I flip us over, settling her beneath me, and grab the still-lit candle she left on the nightstand.

Her lust-filled eyes widen as I hover the candle over her body, almost tilting it, but not quite. Then I pour wax over her full tits, ready for my attention.

She bites her lip as the hot wax rolls on her skin in sync with my thrusts.

"More," she moans.

I grin, loving how much we can push each other. Our sex life is going to be anything but normal—that I know.

I let the wax drip again across her chest, aiming for her left nipple.

When the wax hits the sensitive peak, she arches her back, grabs onto my hand, and digs her nails into me.

"You're so beautiful covered in wax, but now I want you covered in my cum."

"Bury it inside me first, then mark my skin," she says.

"Fuck yes," I groan.

I start pounding her harder, slamming into her depths as her hands rub the wax all over her breasts.

My mouth runs dry at the sight. *How did I ever marry anyone else? How could I have thought there was anyone else for me?*

We are both getting close to exploding when our eyes meet again. We haven't figured everything out, but it doesn't matter in this moment. This moment is about hope—and we both have a lot of it.

"Come with me," I pant.

And we do. We come together, her pussy clenching down, milking me for everything I have.

I fall on top of her, the wax sticking between our bodies. As I stroke her hair, our eyes are serious. We need to have more deep conversations, which will lead to more conflict, which means more destruction of this penthouse suite.

"Did you like that?" I ask.

"Yea..." She scrunches her nose and bites her lip. "But

how do you feel about a foursome? I kind of miss the attention of four men at once."

My face goes white, and she bursts out in laughter underneath me.

I tickle her, not letting her go until she takes it all back.

"I'm kidding! I'm kidding! You're more than enough for me. I don't want other guys or multiple guys. I just want you, only you. Forever you," she says.

19

RI

We fuck all night. We don't dare sleep. I'm not sure we'll ever sleep again anyway. We're too afraid of what will happen if we sleep. *What moments together will we miss? Will this will all be taken from us in a flash?*

It could—it really could.

We haven't talked about tomorrow specifically. We haven't talked about much since we started fucking like our time is running out.

It doesn't matter that we're married; nothing's changed. Every time we're together, it feels like we're about to lose each other all over again. That's what makes this so emotional.

The sun is starting to rise over the strip—another indication of our dwindling time before facing reality.

I'm lying on Beckett's shoulder in one of the many beds in this hotel room. His eyes are closed, but he's not asleep.

I nudge him with my head toward the window. He opens his eyes and sees the hint of yellow climbing over the mountains in the distance.

When he turns his attention back to me, it's with a deep scowl. Tonight was supposed to heal us. It was supposed to mend our wounds and solidify what we mean to each other. It was supposed to be full of promises and plans.

And it was. It was so much more, but our lives are far too complicated to be solved in one night.

Beckett climbs out of bed. "Take a bath with me?"

I nod, and he takes my hand, helping me out of bed. Together we walk naked to the bathroom. Our skin is marked by each other—with cum, with candle wax, with nail scratches, with bruises from our thrusts.

Beckett starts the bathtub and sits on the edge, pulling me into his lap. He strokes my hair gently.

I open my mouth to speak, but he shakes his head. "Not yet."

I nod.

He's right. The most important part of the conversation can wait until the last minute. It won't ruin anything, but it's the most painful topic.

When the tub finishes filling up, Beckett climbs in and helps me sit in front of him.

I lean back against him, relishing feeling him in the warm water while he rubs a bar of soap all over my body.

"I love you," I say, trying not to break.

When we have the conversation, I have no idea what the conclusion will be. Even after the night we had, I'm not sure what he's thinking.

Will he want to end our marriage, end us, in order to save his family and me? Or now that we are together, will he fight with me by his side? Even if it means we, and most likely his family, will die?

I know what my answer is, but I never got him to vow

not to play the hero role. And he never got me to promise not to risk my life to save him. We are both hopeless—hopelessly in love with each other to the point of sacrificing ourselves.

It's not healthy. It's not right, but it's love.

Love is messy. Love is complicated, and love requires sacrifice.

For most people, it means sacrificing a few hours on the weekend to watch a football game even though you hate football. Or go to brunch even though you'd rather sleep in.

But for us, our love requires more.

He pulls me tight against his chest. "I love you too, Queen."

He's called me that a lot lately, but I feel like the nickname is taunting me. I'm not a queen. If I was, we wouldn't be in this predicament. We'd have an army at our disposal to defend our love. Instead, the world is against us.

If I was a queen, I'd have money and power and the ability to control my own fate. Instead, loving him means we'll most likely die in a bloody war.

I sigh.

Beckett kisses the top of my head.

"Okay, it's time," he says, taking a deep, shaky breath.

"You sure?"

"Yes," he says somberly.

There's a pause. Neither of us speaks for a second, each hoping the other will go first.

"I can't live without you," we say at the same time.

I turn and look at Beckett.

"I can't live without you. I won't live without you, not again," he says.

"I can't live without you either, Hero. I won't. No matter

the consequences, I'm tired of hiding. I'm tired of pretending. I'm tired of sacrificing our love to protect each other. We just end up hurt."

He nods even though it kills him to think about losing me. But this way, death will be the only way he'll lose me. He won't be doing it to himself by marrying someone else.

"So we're in this together, forever? No matter what?" he asks.

"I promise. We're in this together—forever."

We kiss—sealing the one promise we can keep to each other. This kiss isn't a battle; it's an orchestrated dance. Our promises slip back and forth to each other until we're content in our vow.

And then, we have to face the reality of our newly made promise far too soon. The second our lips separate, a knock pounds on the door.

We don't have to open it to know what faces us on the other side.

20

BECKETT

We frantically get out of the tub, throw on robes, and grab our guns. We don't need to speak to know what we face. On the other side of that door is most likely a furious Corsi, and he's figured out that I married the wrong daughter.

A battle is about to explode. The Corsi mafia is pissed, the Retribution Kings are pissed, and we are their greatest enemies. *They will both come after us, but who came first?*

The mafia.

Corsi.

I look over at Ri as we walk closer to the door. Last night was incredible, and as much as we got what we needed out of it, it wasn't enough. Only a lifetime together could ever be enough.

We ruined the penthouse suite. Every room is in shatters with broken furniture, shattered glass, and artwork scattered around the floor.

But we started the process of healing ourselves in this room. *Are we about to be broken once again? Are we even going to survive what comes next?*

Ri holds my gaze, clearly thinking all the same things. My worry is mirrored in her face. We are hardly prepared for war—mentally or physically. We're only wearing robes, for goodness sake. *How well can we actually fight in a fucking robe?*

"Together," she whispers, and I remember the promise we made to each other. We're in this together—forever. We will do whatever we have to do to survive and protect each other. Whatever actions we take, we are taking them with the goal of being together forever.

"Forever," I say back.

We both nod. Our love is about to face the ultimate test, but for once, I feel good about our chances.

We approach the door cautiously with our guns aimed at it.

The knock pounds again, angrier and more impatient than last time. I pull back the chair barricade under the door and look through the peephole.

Instantly, my pulse calms.

"It's Lennox," I exhale.

"Fuck," Ri says, her shoulders relaxing.

I quickly unlock and open the door. "What do you want?"

He glares at me as he steps inside with a bag in his hands. "Don't turn off your phone again."

He looks us up and down and shakes his head. "Were you really going to try to take on the mafia or Retribution Kings with a gun and a robe?"

I shrug with a lazy grin.

"You both really are mad."

I put my arm around Ri. "No, we're in love."

Lennox rolls his eyes.

"So, what's the emergency?" Ri asks him.

Lennox frowns, suddenly quiet. "Rialta ran away."

"What do you mean she ran away? She was staying in the same hotel room as the three of you!" Ri yells.

"Yes, and that hotel room is as big as this one. It's basically an entire floor. We didn't think she'd run. We worried about preventing people from coming in, not her escaping."

"How do you know she wasn't kidnapped? Jesus, what was I thinking?" Ri steps out from underneath my shoulder and starts pacing. "I have to find her. I'm supposed to protect her. Fuck, I shouldn't have left her alone."

I grab Ri's shoulder to stop her. "You didn't leave her. Last night was a lot of things, but it wasn't a mistake. Don't ever think that. Ever," I growl.

She nods, and I turn to Lennox, pissed at him for ruining my morning. "Why do you think Rialta snuck out and wasn't kidnapped?"

Lennox reaches into his jacket pocket and pulls out a napkin. He holds it out to us.

Ri grabs it and starts reading aloud.

"Tell River I'm fine, and I'm sorry. I just needed some space to think," Ri reads and sighs, balling up the napkin in her hand.

"We have to go find her," Ri snaps.

"Finding Rialta isn't your biggest problem at the moment. Corsi is furious that Rilata is missing, and he doesn't understand why he can't get ahold of you two," Lennox says.

"Fuck, what did you tell him?" I ask.

"I told him you both went off searching the second you realized she was gone and told us to stay back in case she came back. But I think he's suspicious," Lennox says.

"No, he's just disappointed in me. I've never let him down in almost twenty years, and now I did. He thought I was the perfect protector for her. He thought as long as I was protecting her, she'd be safe. Having a husband to protect her was just added protection," Ri says, running her hand through her hair in frustration.

"So what now?" I ask, looking at Lennox, knowing he already has a plan.

"I told Corsi we'd meet him at the airport to head back to Chicago in an hour."

"Why would we go back if we haven't found Rialta yet?" I ask.

"Because he thinks she went back," Ri says.

"Why would she go back?" I look at Ri.

"Well she wouldn't stay in Las Vegas. If she really ran, she wouldn't make it far. She doesn't have the skills. She doesn't have a fake passport or an endless supply of money. And she's not stupid enough to think she can evade us. She'll be back. There isn't much to do but wait for her, most likely in Chicago, and keep the news quiet," Ri says before glaring at Lennox some more. I want to do more than just glare at Lennox for fucking this up so royally.

Lennox tosses me the bag he's carrying, and I lift an eyebrow.

"Clothes," he explains. "And the plan is simple. You pretend you married Rialta last night. We all got blackout drunk partying and woke up to a missing Rialta. She just got cold feet after reality set in. We are going to meet Corsi on his plane, and the two of you are going to stay as far apart as possible. You don't touch, kiss, or give longing looks to each other. We keep your marriage hidden as long as possible, at least until we find Rialta. After that...well, I hope you two come up with a plan by then."

Ri and I head to one of the bedrooms to get dressed. The clothes Lennox brought are simple—jeans, T-shirts, and tennis shoes. We get dressed quickly, putting our guns in the back of our pants, and all the while, Ri doesn't even look at me. She's too focused on Rialta.

"Hey." I take her hand to get her to finally look at me. "Together."

"Forever," she says in return as if it's our mantra. Maybe if we repeat it enough, it'll be true.

I kiss her now one last time. After we leave this hotel, we can't steal kisses, we can't touch, we can't even look at each other. We have to pretend we hate each other if possible. We have to throw Corsi and his men completely off the scent of what happened last night.

I'm going to enjoy this kiss and take it with me for as long as I need it.

Ri seems to be in agreement as she wraps her arms around my neck and tilts her head to deepen our connection. We cling to each other, pressing our lips together like the oxygen—we need this to survive.

The kiss is too long and too short, all at the same time. We know our time is up at the same time and let go. Our only chance of getting to kiss again is finding Rialta, ensuring my brother and his family's safety, and paying whatever price Corsi inflicts on us for betraying him.

Ri looks down at the wedding ring I put on her finger just last night. She takes it off without hesitation and stows it in her pocket. I hold my hand out to her, link our fingers together, and we head back out to an impatient Lennox.

He frowns when he sees our linked hands but doesn't say anything.

We follow him out into the hotel hallway, our hands dropping the second we leave the threshold of the suite door. It's painful but necessary. We don't look at each other—practice for what's about to come. But I can still see her out of the corner of my eye, and our promise still rings in my ear.

Together—forever.

Downstairs, a car is waiting for us. Gage and Hayes are already in the car. The second we climb in, the driver takes off toward the airport.

"I hope you guys had a good time last night because we all might die for it," Hayes says.

I know he means it as a joke. He's always the one to lighten the mood, but none of us can handle jokes right now. I'm sitting in the back with Lennox. Hayes and Ri sit in the middle, and Gage is sitting upfront with the driver.

Hayes reaches over, taking Ri's hand and giving it a squeeze. I'm jealous he can touch her while I can't. But when she leans her head over onto his shoulder, I realize my jealousy is pointless. I'd sacrifice my happiness for hers a million times over, and I'm thankful a friend can comfort her for a minute when I can't.

We make it to the airport in record time to find the private jet ready and waiting.

I keep my distance from Ri as we head up to the plane. She stops and talks to Corsi at the front of the plane while I head to the back.

Gage sits next to me on the plane with Hayes and Lennox behind me. Ri stays upfront with Corsi, and she doesn't look back. She gives me no indication of what their conversation is about, nothing to tell me if he believes our story or not.

That turmoil is what I endure the entire plane ride back until we land, and I get my answer far too soon.

The second we land, my arm is yanked behind me, and ropes come around my body and ankles. My gun is tossed before I even have a chance to reach for it, a piece of tape is placed over my mouth before I even get a word out.

What. The. Hell?

It happened so fast I didn't have time to react or fight back. I was surrounded by men I thought were my friends, men I considered practically family. And they were the ones who tied me up.

Gage, Hayes, and Lennox all surround me, each aiming a gun at me.

My eyes go to each of them, trying to understand why they did this. Why am I tied up? Why are they aiming a gun at me?

But then I hear the struggle at the front of the plane, and I suddenly no longer care about myself.

"Ri!" I yell, but the sound is muffled by tape.

I can tell by the scuffle of men and the sound of gunfire that Ri saw it coming and fought back. That's not necessarily a good thing—there's a chance she's hurt or dead.

"Ri!" I try again, struggling against the ropes they bound me with, but I can't get free. At least, I won't be able to get out of them fast enough to help Ri.

But it's too late—I see one of Corsi's men hold her up. She breaks the rule Lennox gave us, looking directly at me.

She's tied up in much the same way I am. Her arms are bound behind her, tape is across her mouth, and her ankles are bound together.

"Together," I say even though I know she can't hear me.

"*Forever,*" she says back in my mind.

A single tear falls down my face as I watch her get yanked off the plane and realize how futile our promises are.

A moment after Ri is taken off the plane, Gage and Hayes grab my sides and help me stand before walking me down the aisle of the plane after her. I don't resist. I want to be wherever she is.

And then I spot two blacked-out SUVs, and my heart sinks—we won't be together. To keep our promise of together forever, we're going to have to fight our way back to each other. I have no idea if that will take a day, a week, a year, or a lifetime, but I do know it's a promise I intend to keep.

I'm shoved in the trunk of the second SUV, and I'm sure Ri is currently lying sideways in the back of the one in front of us. I don't know what's happening. I don't know why we are being separated. I don't know what Corsi plans on doing with us.

And I don't know why Lennox, Hayes, and Gage went along with this plan or if they had a choice. Even if they didn't have a choice, they had a chance to warn me.

The car starts moving, and I know I'm being driven away from Ri. I try to calm my breathing, knowing it's not helpful to get upset and worked up. I need to keep my cool to get out of these bindings. I need to solve one problem at a time to get back to her.

Lennox is sitting in the back, leaning behind his seat and looking at me. My eyes shoot daggers into him. When I get free, he'll be the first one I go after.

His face is blank and unreadable, but I swear I hear

him say something—a whisper or maybe it's the wind, or maybe I want to believe that I haven't been betrayed by someone I thought cared about me again. The 'I'm sorry,' whether actually spoken or imagined, is too little too late. I would have accepted my fate if he had made sure Ri was safe. He didn't.

The one thing I have to be thankful for is that Corsi has Ri, not Odette. Corsi is pissed. He'll be angry with Ri —probably even punish her, but he won't kill her. Deep down, Corsi thinks of Ri as a daughter. He cares about her.

I just have to find my way back to her.

21

RI

I HYPERVENTILATE in the back of an SUV as I watch Gage and Hayes lead Beckett out of the plane with Lennox holding a gun at his back. I thought they were his friends. I thought they would do anything to protect him. *What are they doing kidnapping him?*

I thought for a second we might be able to fight our way out of this. We were taken by surprise, but we had three allies at the back, ready to fight with us.

I was wrong.

They lead Beckett to SUV behind mine. We're about to be driven in different directions, taken to different places for Vincent and his men to torture and punish us for what we did.

Separated—this was our nightmare. It's infinitely harder to fight together forever when we're apart. We'll find a way back to each other; we always do—even if we have to go through hell first.

And we will go through hell. Vincent is beyond pissed. I'm sure he figured out the truth by now. My only solace is that he won't kill Beckett. He still needs him to marry Rialta once he finds her.

Although, at the moment, I'm not sure I believe anything that Lennox said. Rialta may be safe and sound; she may have been kidnapped—I have no clue.

The car starts moving, and my heart rips in two—half of it stays with Beckett, while the other keeps me going long enough to get back to him. I'm lying on my right side and can feel the thin metal of my ring digging into my hip, a reminder of who I have to get back to.

I don't know how long we drive, but eventually, the car stops. No one talks in the car, so I don't get many clues about where we are or what Vincent plans on doing with me.

I'm yanked from the back, and my heart sinks. I realize where I am immediately, and everything I thought we face was wrong. I'm carried into the building. I don't fight; there is no use. There are dozens of them and one of me. I'll have to wait to find a time to escape.

I'm carried down the stairs to the center of the arena—an arena I know all too well. The last time I was here, I was tied to a post, and a gun was aimed at my head.

It turns out the pole is still there, and that's where I'm taken. The ropes are loosened enough until one of the men can yank my arms over my head and strap me to the pole. My ankles are still tied, and I still have a piece of tape over my mouth.

I don't think about myself. All I hope for is that Beckett won't be joining me. I'm pretty sure Vincent can be persuaded to let Beckett live as long as he actually agrees to marrying Rialta and keeping her safe, but the Retribution Kings—they don't do forgiveness.

A loud cheer faces my attention around me, seeing every seat filled in the building. I turn my head to the right, already knowing who I'll find walking on stage—Odette and Ryker. I wish I could say I have an ally in Ryker, but I don't—not anymore. The man who once helped me is gone.

They walk onto the stage, hand in hand, no longer hiding their relationship.

I turn my attention from them to the stairs, where I wait for Beckett to be dragged down after me. But after a few minutes pass and he doesn't appear, I realize he isn't coming.

Where is Beckett? What did they do with him? Is he already dead?

My stomach heaves at that thought.

"Welcome everyone, and a very special welcome to our guest, Rialta Corsi," Odette says on the microphone.

I raise my eyebrows. *Really?* She's not even going to use my real name. *She's going to pretend I'm Rialta when she knows I'm not?*

The crowd cheers, but there is also uneasiness in the air. They aren't sure how they feel about their new leader being a woman and hanging out with the leader of another group. Ryker can never be the leader of the Retribution Kings without giving up his claim as leader of the Devil Crew, something I don't think he'll ever do.

"I've gathered you all here today to witness the retribution of Rialta Corsi. She and her family have done untold crimes against my family and me, which means they have committed crimes against all of us. Her family is responsible for my kidnapping, for my rape and torture. They are responsible for taking Beckett away from us—our leader, killed, because of her." A damn tear rolls down her cheek. She's going to play the heartbroken widow card.

Ryker wraps his arm around her and holds her tightly.

"I want to make it clear that Beckett Monroe did nothing wrong. He did what was needed to save and protect me. But this woman and her family—they are the ones in need of eliminating," Odette says.

The frenzied crowd cheers in agreement.

"So what should her retribution be? She's responsible for my kidnapping and torture, for Beckett's kidnapping and death."

I cringe every time she says Beckett is dead. He can't be dead; I'd feel it, right? My heart would know he's gone. If she has him, she stashed him somewhere. She wouldn't kill him so easily.

Me—I'm dead if I don't find a way to escape. I have no allies, no one coming to save me. I have to figure this out myself.

"Death!" the crowd chants over and over again.

Odette smiles, happy with the crowd's request. She and Ryker walk closer to me.

"Then death it shall be," Odette whispers into the microphone.

The crowd falls silent as Ryker hands Odette his gun with coldness in his eyes. Ryker looks at me and asks, "Any last words?"

He doesn't wait for permission from Odette or the crowd. He walks over to me and rips the tape off my mouth in one quick motion, leaving my skin raw and painful.

"Yes, I have some last words," I snap my head back, looking directly at Odette. "For one, I'm not Rialta Corsi."

There are gasps throughout the room.

I have to figure out how to play my cards just right to survive the night.

"My name is River. I'm an orphan that Vincent Corsi took and demanded I play the role of his daughter. He was trying to protect her. I've been their prisoner for most of my life. I've never hurt any of the Retribution Kings. In fact, I helped Beckett every chance I could."

The crowd is hanging onto my every word as I stare down Odette.

Your move.

She looks around, trying to figure out how to handle this. "You did hurt me when you took Beckett from me. You made him play your stupid games. He still died because of you!"

"I'm not loyal to Vincent Corsi. All I did, I did to survive, that was all." And I have to survive now. "Put my loyalty to the test. I can help the Retribution Kings get real retribution against the Corsi mafia. We can end them all once and for all. I know how to get to Vincent, and more importantly, I know how to get to his heir—Rialta Corsi."

The crowd murmurs and Odette's eyes are wild with frustration. She glares in Ryker's direction for a second since he's the one who started this. Her eyes tell me he'll pay for this later.

But then she looks back at me. "Fine. You want to prove yourself loyal to the Retribution Kings?"

I nod.

"You put Beckett through hell to win Rialta, only to kill him the second he won. We, Retribution Kings, are more honest. When we make a deal, we keep it," she says.

"Same," I reply.

She laughs at that.

"Fine, we'll give you a challenge soon. Show us how

badly you want to be loyal to us. Show us how badly you are sorry for your part in Beckett's death. If you survive, then you will be one of us. Then we will see if the information you have is true," Odette says.

Odette turns off the mic and starts walking off the stage, Ryker trailing behind her.

I survived to live a little longer, but not much longer. Whatever task Odette creates will be sure to have one outcome—my death. All I've done is just prolong it a little longer.

But her words haunt me. Is Beckett alive or dead? She speaks with so much certainty about his death—she knows if he isn't already dead, he will be soon.

22

BECKETT

"You didn't keep your word," Vincent Corsi says as I come to.

I'm in a dark dungeon, my body still bound as I kneel in front of him like he's some sort of king.

"I did, actually," I grumble.

He frowns. "You're married to my daughter, Rialta Corsi?"

"No, but I never said I would marry Rialta Corsi. The agreement we shook on was that I would marry your daughter."

"Rialta is my only daughter," he snaps.

"Is she? I'm pretty sure you have an adopted daughter. And if you didn't legally adopt her, you can't deny that you care about her. River Corsi is just as much your daughter as Rialta Corsi."

Corsi doesn't answer me. He doesn't dispute my claim, confirming the truth. But I don't know what that means for Ri or me.

"Where is Ri?" I ask.

Corsi stares me down, and I assume he's going to answer me. But when he finally does, it's not much of an answer. "Being punished," he says.

I frown. "This isn't her fault! She did nothing wrong! She didn't plan it; Rialta did. And she would have done anything for her sister, anything for you."

"She failed to keep Rilata safe," he barks.

"Rialta's safe; she's just on the run. She needed space because she didn't want to be forced to marry someone she didn't choose," I say.

Corsi's jaw ticks, but he doesn't say anything. That single tick tells me a lot, though—there is definitely more to Rialta than I know.

I narrow my eyes at Corsi. It's almost like he's trying to tell me something but can't.

From the corner of my eye, I see who else is in the dungeon with me—Lennox, Hayes, and Gage.

"What now?" I ask Corsi, assuming I'm about to be tortured until I agree to marry Rialta. But I don't know what part the three behind me played in all of this.

"Now, you'll be punished," he says. Without warning, Corsi pulls his gun out and shoots me three times.

I fall to the floor, numb and most likely dying.

"You can tell Odette it's done. I'll send the video proof soon," Corsi says.

The room is going black, but my eyes are open enough to see three sets of feet walk past me.

Tell Odette it's done.

It hits me all at once—Ri is with Odette. And Corsi did this under Odette's orders to trade for his daughter's life. Corsi would never work with Odette and the Retribution Kings, but he would do anything to keep his daughter safe.

But which daughter is he protecting?

I gasp, the pain in my chest overtaking me, knowing I'll probably never figure it out.

23

RI

I'M LEFT TIED to the pole for hours while Odette decides what challenge I'm going to endure before my death. I haven't accepted my fate—not yet, but it is a strong possibility that all of this ends in my death. However, that's something I'll gladly welcome if Beckett is indeed dead.

This isn't the first time I've worried about Beckett dying, but I've never been so close to getting everything I've ever wanted—so fucking close to getting my happily ever after.

All I've thought about the entire time I've been tied here is him. Trying to figure out if he's alive or dead. Trying to figure out if I still have a future with him. Trying to figure out what Odette would get from lying.

She probably told me to break me, but I'm not going to let her. I won't give in until I see Beckett's lifeless body with my own eyes. I refuse to believe he's dead, not after everything we've been through.

"Are you done crying yet?" Odette asks, walking back on stage in the empty arena with a dozen men behind her.

I stare her down. "You really think these men are going

to stay loyal to you? They're called Retribution Kings. There is no room in their world for a queen to be in charge." I hate that it's true, but it is. The men will soon rally around another man. They won't let Odette keep her power once she kills me, and they confirm Beckett is really dead. Her days are numbered.

She smirks. "Let's see how smart your mouth is after what I have in store for you." She snaps her fingers at the men behind her. Two of them glare at her; one rolls his eyes at her.

Yea, she's definitely losing them already. But they obey her, for now. Three men walk over to me and start untying me from the pole.

"Where's your boyfriend? Is he in timeout after he helped me?" I ask as the ropes come down from the pole, and my up-stretched shoulders finally get relief.

She glares at me, and I can practically see the steam shooting out her nostrils. If I'm going to die, it gives me satisfaction to get under her skin first.

"You have to survive everything you've put Beckett and me through. I doubt you'll survive the night; neither did Beckett," she says.

I pull on the ropes as the men jerk me into a standing position.

"What did you do to Beckett?" I ask.

She folds her arms across her chest and raises an eyebrow, realizing how to get under my skin—taunting me with news about Beckett.

"Survive tonight, and maybe I'll tell you." She licks her lips, looking at me like I'm her meal. "I should thank Ryker for sparing your life. Killing you quickly would have been too merciful. I'm going to enjoy torturing you."

She nods at the three men holding onto me, and they

yank on the ropes around my wrists, pulling me off the stage and up the arena stairs. I don't look back at Odette to see what she's doing—I don't give her the satisfaction. I have to put all my focus on surviving what's next—at least until I find out if Beckett is alive or dead.

She better pray he's alive. If he's dead, she hasn't seen how dangerous I can be.

We walk to a hotel—the same hotel where I had to listen to Beckett and Odette fuck.

The three men drag me into the exact same room as that night. I know she's going to come. She can't resist watching.

"I thought this room would work the best. I have lots of happy memories in this room," Odette says from the doorway, her hand running up and down the doorframe nostalgically.

I remember how I felt listening to them having sex, but I realize now that it wasn't fucking, it wasn't lovemaking—it was rape. She forced him to have sex with her.

"You raped him in here," I say.

One of the guys looks at me carefully, not sure he heard me right.

I pull against the ropes, trying to approach her, but the men hold me back. "You raped Beckett here. He wouldn't have ever touched you otherwise. He loves me, not you. You lied to him every step of the way. All you ever wanted was revenge."

"Revenge is who I am. It's who I was born to be. That's what the Retribution Kings care about—revenge," Odette says.

"Maybe, but do I deserve revenge for loving the man you manipulated? That's all I'm guilty of—loving him."

"You're guilty of a heck of a lot more," she snaps back.

I shrug. "I guess technically I did marry him."

Odette's mouth falls. "You bitch. Hold her down and remove her clothes." She slams the door behind her as she gives the order.

Two of the men act immediately, the third takes a second to snap to it, but eventually, all three men are yanking at my clothes and trying to get me onto the bed. I have no doubt what these men and Odette plan on doing to me, and it's something I won't allow.

My shirt is ripped down the middle, my pants are shimmied down my hips, and my bra is undone from the back. I want to fight back immediately. I want to stop them from even removing my clothes, but the best way to beat them is to wait, be patient, and work on the ropes.

While I let my outer facial expression appear frantic and terrified, I calmly lower my heart rate and breathing so I can focus on getting out of the ropes.

Unfortunately, the opportunity to escape doesn't come until the men have removed all of my clothes and slammed me down onto the bed with my arms pulled over my head once again. My ankles are thankfully still tied together.

Odette steps forward, towering over me with a sneer. "Not so tough and sassy now, are you?"

I let my bottom lip tremble a little, anything to make me look small and meek.

"A mafia princess—that's what you masqueraded as. You used tricks and deception to get Beckett to fall for you. You used your pretend mafia father to force him to marry you. You wanted to destroy the Retribution Kings and me; that was your assignment. You're nothing but a dirty, little slut. You're a princess of nothing. And my men are about to remind you of your place in the world."

Odette looks to the three men tying me down. "Do as you want with her. Touch her. Fuck her. Torture her. Make her wish she was never born."

She sits back in the chair in the corner, happy to enjoy the show.

She's going to get a show alright, but not the one she's expecting.

The men hesitate for a second. Removing my clothes is one thing; actually raping me is a whole other.

Soon I feel a hand squeeze my boob, then another hand. Once they get started, their confidence will build, and they'll have no problem raping me by the end.

Another hand grabs for my neck, and that's when I whisper, "Please."

His hand squeezes harder, most likely bruising my neck, while the other hands mark my boobs.

I cry out, and the sound I make isn't fake; the pain is real. I can barely breathe as the hand tightens on my neck. And the man squeezing my nipple has about pulled it off, while the third has dug his claws so deep into my flesh, I'll have permanent marks on my breast.

Because of their hesitation, I was going to let them live. But now they've shown me they're just as big of monsters as her, so they all get to die.

I have to endure more than I want. I have to endure their groping, sloppy kisses, and bites along my body. One touch between my legs is almost my undoing.

I'm patient, though. My time is coming. Soon they'll be dead on the floor for what they've done.

"Had enough yet?" Odette asks in a high-pitched voice from her corner chair. I almost forgot she's still here.

Another hand slides between my thighs. Tears burn my eyes, but I don't let them out. Nor do I let out the cry in the back of my throat. And I definitely don't let out the retort that would tell her I'm not broken—not even close.

"Spread her legs and let's see how long it takes to break her," Odette says.

I hold my breath, waiting for the moment the knife slices the ropes on my ankles free. It seems to take the man forever to saw slowly on the ropes, but I'm ready for the exact moment I'm free. I won't let them hold me or touch me a second longer.

The second the rope breaks in two, I make my move. My hands slip through the ropes at my wrists that I've been loosening. The guy strangling my throat gets a quick punch to the eye from me while I kick the guy who just cut me free in the eyeball.

The third reaches for his gun—excellent. He shoots, but too late—I'm already rolling into him. I knock the gun free and shoot him in the chest before he has time to react. Two more shots, and the other two men are down.

I aim the gun at the corner chair, but Odette's long gone.

I frown, pulling the rest of the rope off my wrists and ankles before climbing out of bed.

I'm still naked, but I don't give a damn about modesty. I have to get out of here before Odette sends more men to stop me.

I run to the door, throw it open, and am faced with a gun pointed at my head.

"I got her," Lennox says.

"Where's Beckett?" I ask immediately. He was the one who took him. He's half the reason I'm here.

He doesn't answer. Although his throat bobs up and down and his mouth opens as if he wants to speak but can't.

I'm pissed at him. He deserves to die for what he did. I still have a gun in my hand, and I know I could take him. But even if he deserves to die, I'm not sure I can do it, not yet. But I have no problem bringing him close to death.

I duck and charge at him.

He simply steps out of the way, and I run straight into Hayes's and Gage's arms. The gun is knocked from my hand, and sharp metal handcuffs are clasped on my wrists as my arms are yanked behind my body.

They push me back into the bedroom while Lennox keeps his gun on me.

"You're all going to die for this!" I scream.

"Don't worry. Unlike the others, we won't underestimate how dangerous you are, Princess," Hayes says.

Odette steps back into the room. "Clean this up and make sure she's thoroughly broken by morning time," she orders.

And then she leaves, too much of a coward to stay. She's too afraid I'll get free again and kill her like I did the others.

I look from one man to the next, hating them all. "Don't you dare touch me."

None of them speak as they approach me, and I squirm against my restraints. I may have let them fuck me before, but there is no way I'm letting these guys touch me now. The only problem is the guys that tried before weren't prepared—these guys are. I'm not sure I can get out of here unscathed.

Lennox is still holding his gun on me. Hayes is moving closer with a smirk on his face and an eagerness in his eyes. But it's Gage who catches me off guard when I feel the sharpness of a needle plunged into my neck before blackness consumes me.

24

RI

"Wake up, Princess," Odette's voice rings in my head. A crowd laughs nearby, and I know I'm back in that damn arena again. Once again, I'm tied to the pole, but this time I'm sore, so fucking sore.

My head throbs with the power of a migraine. But it's not just my head and the drugs inflicting pain—I hurt everywhere. I look down at my body and realize I'm still naked. What bothers me are the bruises and cuts that weren't there before. The most I remember is having some rope burn around my wrists—but this happened after the drugs knocked me out.

I feel violated. I have no idea if I was raped or assaulted, but I was tortured. You don't get bruises like these without being tortured—and I know the three guys responsible.

I look up and find all three of them standing behind Odette like they've been loyal to her this entire time.

Fuck, Beckett and I really screwed up who we trusted. I won't be making that mistake again.

Ryker is on the stage too but isn't next to Odette.

Instead, he has a gun aimed at a hooded man bound to a chair.

Beckett?

My heart thumps loudly, hoping it's him. But quickly, I realize it's not Beckett. This man has two arms, and my heart doesn't recognize his presence like it does Beckett.

"There you are. We thought you were going to sleep forever," Odette says with a laugh.

My brain is spinning with what to do, but this is a difficult situation to get out of without help. There are too many people for me to take down on my own. And I don't know if anyone is coming to my aid.

Together—forever.

Our promise to each other rings in my head. I'm not going to let this be the end. I'm going to find a way to keep my promise. It's the only promise I made to Beckett, and he made to me. He has to be alive. Wherever he is, he's fighting to get back to me, and that's what I'll do too. I'll fight until the very end.

"Have you had enough yet? Do you surrender? If so, I'll show mercy and put you out of your misery," Odette says, stepping right in front of me, waiting for me to answer.

"You haven't broken me. You think some bruises broke me?" I laugh. "You don't know who I am. I'm River Corsi. I was raised by Vincent Corsi and taught how to kill by Kek. I was brought up as a princess but also as a warrior. I wear a pretty dress and still kick all of your asses at the same time. You don't get to break me. I won't let you."

Odette narrows her eyes, crouching down to my eye level. "You may have been taught to withstand torture, but I can promise you from experience that someday that pain will catch up to you if you live long enough for the nightmares to start. In the meantime, let's try a different kind of torture, one to elicit a very different effect on you."

She turns and looks at the three men I thought were my allies but were actually my biggest enemies. They all walk over to me. Lennox starts undoing my ropes. He doesn't just untie me from the pole, but he unties my wrists completely. Gage unties the ropes at my ankles too.

"Going to drug me again so you can rape me?" I snap.

None of them answer. They don't even look at me.

Lennox grabs my wrists and yanks me to my feet. I don't have to look behind me to know Hayes has a gun pointed at me. They walk me over to within ten feet of the seated, hooded man.

I know—I know what they are going to ask me to do.

Ryker walks over to me. He empties his gun, leaving only one bullet, and then hands it to me with a solemn look. He walks back to Odette's side while the three Retribution Kings all aim their guns at me, ensuring I can't turn the gun on any of them.

"So you want to be a Retribution King?" Odette asks. "Then we have one initiation task for you. Can you seek retribution yourself?" The room quiets, waiting to see what I'm going to do.

"This man in front of you deserves to die for what he did. You have a single shot in that gun. Kill him, and you will be one of us," she finishes.

It's not that simple. Even if I did kill this man, she would never let me be one of them. She'd never just let me walk free.

"Who is he?" I ask.

"Does it matter? You want to be one of us; then you kill him. You'll be getting retribution for me; that's all you need to know," she snaps.

You'll be getting retribution for me.

I stare at the man. He hasn't moved, he hasn't squirmed, he hasn't fought to get free at all. He's been drugged. He probably isn't even awake. It might be a more merciful way to die, but this man doesn't deserve death.

I know who this man is based on her words—Beckett's brother, Enzo Black.

I don't know how the Retribution Kings got him. I thought Vincent had him and his family tucked safely away, but it proves the Retribution Kings are more powerful than I thought.

"And if I don't kill him?" I ask.

"Then they'll kill you," Odette says.

I figured as much.

"Where is Beckett?" I ask, looking at Odette.

"Kill him, and I'll tell you," she says.

"No. I'm done playing games. Tell me where Beckett is," I demand.

Odette sighs, looking bored. "I already told you, he's dead."

"I don't believe you."

"That's not really my problem. All you can do is save yourself."

"You want me to kill this man? You want me to crumble and break and become yours, then give me proof that Beckett is dead."

Odette stares at me for a second, considering my words. Then she turns to Hayes and gives him a nod.

Hayes frowns and walks forward hesitantly. For some reason, he doesn't want to show me the proof. Each step he takes toward me, my heart beats faster.

This can't be happening.

But I don't know why Hayes would be walking toward me if he didn't have proof.

He pulls out his phone.

No.

No, no, no!

He turns the screen toward me, and then he presses play.

Vincent is standing in front of a kneeling Beckett. The next second, three shots are fired. I've seen Vincent kill so many men like that, but never someone I loved.

One second the shots are fired; the next, Beckett is collapsed on the floor.

I tear my eyes away almost immediately.

It can't be true. It could be a fake video.

I look up at Hayes. I look into his eyes—all I see is heartbreak. Whoever they are loyal to and why, I don't know, but Hayes at least cared about Beckett.

And Hayes believes Beckett is dead.

"I'm sorry. I was there. He's dead," Hayes says in a whisper only I can hear.

The grief is instant, but I don't break down like I thought I would. I don't collapse and fall to my knees, giving up. That's not how I'm hardwired. All the training and hypnosis of my childhood take over, and all I can think about is revenge.

Maybe I'd be a better Retribution King than anyone thinks. Instantly, I know what I have to do.

Together—forever.

I'll be joining Beckett soon enough, but first...

I turn toward the man seated in the chair.

"Save yourself and kill your lover's brother or join the man you love in death, which will it be?" Odette says in hushed tones. Only those on stage heard her.

I raise the gun with a shaky hand and aim it at Enzo.

I fire.

The crowd gasps, all eyes on Enzo.

"I missed. I want to try again," I say.

I can feel Odette smirking behind me. "Hayes, give her your gun," she says.

Hayes hands it to me instantly, and now I'm the one smirking. I spin and start firing at Odette. I'm not going to survive long in a crowd of people that want me dead, but I just have to survive long enough to kill one asshole.

25

RI

I REALIZE the second I shoot why Odette wasn't afraid to let me hold a loaded gun. Ryker dives in front of her, taking the bullet meant for her.

I cringe, wishing he wouldn't have done that, but people do crazy things when they're in love. Odette knew Ryker loved her—he'd do anything for her.

I understand the emotion. Even though Beckett's gone, I'd still do anything for him, including fighting a war I can't win.

Odette made one very important mistake, though. When she ordered Hayes to hand me a gun, she didn't think to have him remove all but one bullet first. So even though Ryker protected her, she has no protection against the next bullet I send her way or the one after that.

I don't let her have any last words. I don't play my revenge slow and sweet. I just kill her with a bullet to the head and watch her corpse fall to the floor.

I turn around to find the stage being swarmed with men all aiming their guns at me. I don't know how many bullets I have left, but I'll kill as many of them as I can.

I start firing.

I should run, but I'm not sure I can survive the heartbreak. I should live for Rialta. I should live to protect her, wherever she is, but I can't. I can't live for other people, not anymore.

I've always thought I'd die fighting for someone I loved. I thought that person would be Rialta, but it turns out it's Beckett.

I shoot over and over again as bullets fly past me. Thankfully, their aim is horrible, but I quickly run out of bullets. Still, I don't run—not even when a man runs directly at me.

I punch him hard in the gut, but it's not enough. He wraps his arms around me and lifts me off my feet before jumping off the stage.

"Let me go!" I yell, but the man doesn't stop running, his grip on me unyielding. He just keeps running, and damn, is he fast. His scent is also familiar, but I can't place it.

He runs outside and across streets until we are deep in the nearby forest. Only then does he put me down. The second he lets go, I throw him a punch and a kick, knocking him to the ground. I jump on top of him, reaching for his gun and aiming it at his head.

He puts his hands up.

"Whoa, I'm thankful you missed before, but I know you won't miss from this close. I might want you to shoot me, though, if what they said is true. Is Beckett dead?" the man asks.

My shoulders slump, and I lower the gun. "Enzo?"

He nods. "Is he dead?"

"Yes," I whisper.

I collapse, and Enzo catches me, keeping me from falling onto the ground. We sit, facing each other.

I take a moment to study his features. He's similar to Beckett in a lot of ways, but also so different. They share the same dark hair, eyes, build, and even smell.

But Enzo has an easiness around him. He's a man who has found his purpose, his love, his life. He's a man who has lived a full life and still has people to live for.

"I'm sorry. I should have protected him. I shouldn't have married him. I shouldn't have—"

Enzo wraps his arms around me. "Just as I should have protected him. He's my brother, and I failed."

"He's my husband, and I failed."

The tears start on both of us. "Fuck!" I yell.

"Fuck!" Enzo yells.

The release isn't enough for either of us, but we can't stay here, not with so many people after us. I couldn't protect Beckett, but I can at least keep his brother safe. That's what Beckett cared about most.

I jump up, wipe my tears on the back of my arm, and hold out my hand to him. He takes it and removes his shirt, handing it to me.

I slip it on, grateful for its length covering my ass.

"We need to get you out of here. Beckett wanted to know you're safe," I say.

"He wanted to know you're safe, too," Enzo says.

"I'm not sure I can leave."

"I understand, but I'm not leaving you here. You can come with me, or I can take you anywhere you want to go, but I won't leave you here."

I nod. "I want to go home."

I need to know if Rialta is safe, and I still have revenge

I need to finish for Beckett. Plus, I can't be with this man that smells so much like Beckett—I'll break completely.

We run through the woods until we reach a car. Enzo jumps it and drives; I'm too shaken up to even consider driving. He doesn't ask me for directions, somehow knowing how to get to Vincent's headquarters.

I'm thankful. I'm not in the mood to talk or think or anything.

Once we get close, Enzo decides it's time to talk. "I know you aren't ready, and you may never be ready to meet us—Beckett's family—but if and when you are, we're here. We would love to get to know the woman Beckett loved so fiercely. He risked everything for you."

I shake my head. "You don't want to meet the woman responsible for his death and for almost getting you and your family killed."

Enzo takes my hand and gives it a squeeze. "You aren't responsible for his death. You're responsible for his life—for him finding something worth fighting for. I've only just met you, but I know exactly why you're the woman for him. Unlike the other women Beckett fell for—you're the real deal." He stops the car and lets go of my hand. "And I owe you; you saved my life. I'd be dead too if it wasn't for you."

"I'm so sorry," I say.

"Me too."

He reaches over and hugs me.

I hug him back, but it's painful. It leaves me needing more, but no hug in the world is enough right now.

He eventually lets go.

"I'm not leaving town until I know you're okay. But go be with your family right now. I'll find you out before I leave," he says.

I nod and climb out of the car, heading into the warehouse building Vincent uses as mafia headquarters.

Enzo thinks I'm here to be with family, to heal. Really, I'm here to take down Vincent for killing the man I love. And once I do that, the mafia won't let me survive.

I march into the spacious room filled with Vincent's men.

"Where is he?" I ask, to no one in particular.

One of the men points toward the front of the room.

I'm laser-focused as I walk toward Vincent. All I see is him.

I don't have a weapon. I'm only wearing a T-shirt. I should have thought my plan through more, but it doesn't matter—Vincent Corsi is a dead man.

"Thank god!"

That voice.

I turn and see Rialta running toward me. She tackles me with a hug, wrapping her arms around me.

"I was so terrified, but I should have known that River Corsi always survives," she says.

She tightens her grip on me, and finally, I hug her back.

It's good to know she's okay before I kill Vincent. I'll die knowing she's alive. I don't know who will be left to protect her. Unfortunately, the mafia will choose someone for her to marry that will continue Vincent's horrible legacy, but that was always her fate as long as she stayed.

I hug her tighter before my eyes turn back to Vincent. But then I see the men sitting at his table talking to him—Retribution Kings.

Gage, Hayes, and Lennox.

I take a deep breath as I let go of Rialta, my plan changing. I'll kill them all with my bare hands.

I start running toward them with that intention when nearby doors open suddenly. My breath catches in my throat as Beckett is pushed out into the room.

26

BECKETT

"They were just bags; it can't hurt that bad," Corsi says.

I blink, my entire torso throbbing. But I look down and realize I'm free of restraints and there is no blood, just my badly bruised body.

"It still hurts like a motherfucker," I say.

"I'm sure. But if you're going to stay married to my daughter, you'll have to get used to a little pain."

I raise my eyebrows as I pull myself back into a sitting position. "You're going to let me stay married to Ri?"

"I don't have a choice. It seems she's chosen you. And as you said, I've come to think of her like a daughter too, as much as I tried to keep it a strictly business relationship. I tried for years to be the ruthless mafia leader everyone feared, including her. But she was never afraid of me, even when she was hypnotized and didn't remember everything. Why? I loved her and was never as cruel as I needed to be to her," Corsi says.

"You were pretty cruel. You made her play a horrible game where she thought she was going to have to marry a monster at the end of it."

"Well, I could have been worse."

I lift my shirt, looking down at the bruises on my chest. Even though it hurts, he somehow missed hitting every vital organ. If the bags did penetrate my skin, I wouldn't have died from any of the shots.

"Good shooting," I say, surprised.

"Who do you think taught Ri how to shoot?"

I grin. "So what now?"

Vincent turns serious. "Now, hopefully, your men have rescued both of my daughters."

"My men?"

"The Retribution Kings."

"You mean Lennox, Gage, and Hayes?"

He nods.

"I thought—"

"They're still loyal to you, although probably currently devastated that you died."

"If they are on my side, then why did you let them think I died?"

"They aren't very good actors, and I need the rest of them to think you're dead."

"Why?" I ask, annoyed.

"Those were the terms to get Rialta back."

"The Retribution Kings have Rialta?"

"She'll be free soon when they show Odette the video of your death, and she sees how heartbroken your men are."

"And Ri?" I ask.

Vincent gets quiet.

I jump up. "What the hell happened to Ri?"

"Odette has her but have a little faith. Ri is the strongest person we both know; she'll survive. She always does."

"And if not?"

"I have a team ready to go in and get her as soon as Rialta is secured."

"So you're putting Rialta's life above Ri's once again?"

"No, I'm giving both of my daughters the best chance of survival."

"I'll go. Let me lead the team."

"Actually, you need to do something else first."

"What?" I ask. I'm really getting annoyed pulling teeth with this jackass.

"While you've earned my forgiveness, you need to earn the rest of the mafia's if you want to live."

"They still want me as your replacement?"

"No, Rialta is my heir. They won't recognize Ri as my heir, even if I see her as my daughter. They see what you did to Rialta as a betrayal. It leaves us all in the same situation as before—no husband or future heir to step into my shoes."

"Why don't you just choose someone in the mafia?"

"For one, there aren't many men anywhere near Rialta's age. And two, it just causes infighting. It's better to marry outside the family."

"It's not going to be me," I snap.

"I know that."

"So, what do I have to do?"

Hours pass, but finally, Corsi's men come to get me. They don't tie me up, but they roughly drag my bruised body out of the dungeon and up to the main floor. They shove me hard into a room filled with mafia men.

But my eyes only care about one person—Ri.

We run to each other, and she jumps at me uncontrollably, knocking me to the floor.

"You're alive!" she says.

"So are you," I say, in awe of her as always.

"Together," she whispers.

"Forever."

And then she kisses me—a hard, fast kiss. "I thought you were dead."

"Never."

The room is silent as they watch us, and I know what I have to do. Slowly, we stand up. No guns are pointed at us, but there might as well be.

"So what now?" Ri asks, intertwining our fingers. "Do we kill Lennox and the others?"

I stare at her, realizing she doesn't know the truth. "No, they were just trying to save Rialta and keep us safe."

She turns to me. "Are you sure?"

I nod.

"Thank god, I really didn't want to kill them."

I laugh at that. "No, you really didn't want to think your judgment in people was that off."

We get up off the floor, and I turn to the crowd.

"Now, I need to apologize to all of you. I need to apologize because I fought for the right to marry your princess and become your leader. I thought that's what I wanted, but I was wrong." I look to Ri.

"I fell in love with this woman you all know: a strong, fierce woman—my equal in every way. I fell in love even when I shouldn't have. I fell in love with her again and again and again." I squeeze her hand.

"I know I agreed to marry Rialta Corsi and become the new heir, but I can't. I'm in love with River. You deserve to have a leader who is devoted to you, not in love with someone else."

"You can have a whore on the side and still marry Rialta. A lot of us do!" someone shouts from the crowd. Many of the men chuckle their response.

Ri scrunches her nose at that thought, and I'm sure Rialta thinks much the same.

"I'm sorry, but I can't be the heir."

The crowd breaks out into a cacophony of objections.

"You won! That was the deal!"

"You don't get to back out! If you do, you die; it's the mafia way."

"Kill him; he knows too much!"

Ri tries to step in front of me, but I won't let her. "Together," I whisper, holding her at my side. If they are going to kill us, then they can kill us side by side. I refuse to let her save me, and I know she won't let me save her.

"Forever," she smiles back.

We will fight them together until our last breaths. If that is to be our retribution for falling in love, then so be it. We would both fall in love with each other again and again, even if it only meant brief moments of happiness together.

"Wait!" Corsi says, suddenly, stepping in front of us. "Don't kill them!"

The men lower their guns.

"They are both the best fighters any of us have ever seen. Beckett's talents would be wasted as the leader. He's a much better soldier. And you've all seen River's skills. They need to be protecting, not leading," he says.

I don't disagree with that. Although, I'm not sure I want to spend my life protecting Rialta and whatever bastard she ends up marrying. But that's a battle for another day. As long as I get to be with River, that's all that matters to me.

There's some mumbling, but the crowd seems to agree with Vincent's assessment.

"But who will marry Rialta then? Who will be your heir? She's twenty-one. It's time to find the next heir," someone says from the crowd.

"It just so happens I got an offer I think would make a perfect husband to Rialta and a great mob boss. But, of course, we need to put him to the test first," Vincent says.

The crowd seems to agree with Vincent, but before we can hear who it is, Ri pulls me out of the room and back into the hallway, away from any man who decides to take matters into their own hands and shoot us as traitors.

She touches me all over my chest. "You're alive."

I grin. "You seem surprised?"

"I just expected to be the one to rescue you; I am your hero after all," she says with a sly smile.

"That you are." I kiss her, dipping her back. "You're also my wife, my forever, the love of my life."

She giggles.

"But I'd really like you to put some pants on. I'm tired of everyone seeing your legs."

"Is that so? I was thinking pants won't be necessary for what I have planned next." Her eyes twinkle with sultry sin.

I bite down on my bottom lip, growling. "I want to do just that, but first, I need to know we're okay. Are you okay with what Vincent proposed?"

"I will always protect Rialta, just like you will always protect your family."

I nod, looking her over. "Did Odette hurt you?"

The door opens again, and the Retribution Kings join us in the hallway.

"Technically, that was us. Sorry," Hayes says. "We knocked you out so you'd feel less of the pain. And I promise, we didn't touch you anywhere inappropriate," Hayes says.

"You did this to her?" I fume.

Hayes nods.

I punch him. Then Gage. Then Lennox.

"Thank you for doing what you could to protect her and Rialta," I say.

"Thank you for not being dead," Hayes says.

"And thank you for killing Odette," Gage says to Ri.

"You killed Odette?" I ask her.

She nods.

"Badass." I kiss her firmly. "Thank god."

She smiles somberly. Killing someone never feels good, even someone that deserves to die.

"You need to call your brother!" she says suddenly. "He thinks you're dead."

"Already called him. He's on his way over right now," Rialta says with a sad smile as she steps into the hallway.

I don't know why she's upset. I don't know who her father is going to make her marry, and I don't care. Right now, all I care about is Ri.

I grab Ri, lifting her up until her legs are wrapped around me. "I need you, now."

I start carrying her down the hallway, happy to fuck her in the first room I can find. Apparently, it's a bathroom. I flick the door locked behind us as my mouth descends on hers, remembering our bathroom encounter after her group fucking with the guys.

"Together," I whisper into her mouth.

"And forever," she bites back against my lip.
I grin. Our forever is going to last a long time.

EPILOGUE
RI

BECKETT GRABS my hand and leads me out of the galley where Kai, my sister-in-law, and Enzo, my brother-in-law, are busy cooking dinner for everyone. I love spending time on their yacht with them.

I've loved getting to know his family, but we never get much time together alone when we're here. At least, not enough time for us. Just fucking in our bedroom at night isn't enough, so I'm glad Beckett leads me away from people onto the main deck and then up more stairs.

I raise an eyebrow. "Shouldn't we be sneaking off to our room?"

"This is way more fun," Beckett says as he yanks me to him and kisses me like it's our first and last kiss. It's the way he always kisses me.

I smile against his lips. I've been doing a lot of grinning the last few weeks.

Grinning because I have him, and the personal threats against us are gone.

Grinning because Vincent finally told me he loves me and considers me a daughter.

Grinning because of how great Beckett's family is.

Grinning because the Retribution Kings are no longer a threat to us while they decide their next leader.

Grinning because keeping Rialta safe keeps us occupied and gives us a purpose greater than ourselves.

Grinning because being able to fuck Beckett whenever I want is the greatest thing I've ever experienced.

His hand slides up my thigh under my dress. "Have I told you how much I love it when you wear a dress?"

I laugh as he palms my bare ass. "It's the only reason I wear dresses."

He grins against my lips as his hand slides around my thigh, finding my knife. He grabs it and flings it away, sticking it into the railing.

I laugh. "What? You don't like it when I hold a knife against your throat while I fuck you?"

"As much as I love it when you mark my body, I much prefer marking yours more." His teeth come down on my bare shoulder, and I moan as he pretends to suck my blood like a vampire.

"I'm sure you do." I reach into his pants and pull out his cock, wrapping my hand around it and pumping him.

He groans at my touch, letting his head fall back.

I smirk, knowing I have control now.

I slide down his body until I'm on my knees in front of him and put his cock in my mouth.

His hand immediately fists my hair, trying to dictate my movements. But as I take him down my throat, he has no control, no power—it's all me.

Before I can make him come, he yanks on my hair so hard his cock pops out of my throat. That's when the battle begins.

Somehow my dress gets ripped in two.

His shirt gets thrown overboard.

We break the couch we didn't notice at first.

We're both bleeding, sweaty, and covered in each other's cum by the time we're done.

"Will you two stop breaking all our furniture and fucking where everyone can see you?" Enzo says.

I laugh against Beckett's chest as we sit curled up on the floor of the top deck.

"I'll pay you back for the furniture, but I told you we needed a longer honeymoon," Beckett replies.

"We let you borrow a yacht for a month. You'd think that would be long enough," Enzo shouts back.

"Forever won't be long enough," Beckett pants.

"Just get back down here—with some clothes on. Dinner's finished, and the kids have been traumatized enough," Enzo says.

"If you don't want us naked, you're going to have to toss some clothes up," Beckett says.

Immediately some clothes hit us each in the face. I grin—apparently, Enzo was prepared for this situation.

"Speaking of babies," I say, wiggling my eyebrows.

"Are you finally ready to take a pregnancy test?" Beckett asks.

"No." I stare down at my stomach. "But I'm close."

I haven't had a period in weeks. I have no idea if I'm pregnant or not. Honestly, I'm not sure how I feel. *Do I want kids? Can kids even be a part of our lives if we are constantly going to be protecting, always putting ourselves into harm's way?*

I don't know.

And if we are pregnant, would Rialta understand if we can't be her main protectors anymore?

I don't know.

"Whether I am or not, we'll figure it out together," I say.

He kisses my forehead. "That we will."

There are unlimited dangers out there still. The most important task is trying to figure out who has wanted Rialta dead all these years. It's someone on the inside, someone that knows too much.

They succeeded in killing every member of Vincent Corsi's family except her, and they'll keep trying. Until we figure it out, we'll do our best to keep her safe. Just like we keep each other safe, and just like our families protect us.

We get dressed and head downstairs for dinner. We all barely fit around the table. Enzo and Kai, Zeke and Siren, Langston and Liesel, and all of their kids are here—all members of Beckett's family. Hayes, Gage, and Lennox are here too. They've become family to both of us.

Lastly, Rialta beams at me from her place at the table.

I sit down with Beckett to my left and Rialta on my right, who is seated next to Lennox.

"He's insufferable," Rialta says, not caring if he overhears her.

"I thought you liked him?" I ask.

"Father is crazy if he thinks I'll marry him."

I look from her to Lennox, who doesn't seem the least bit phased as he drinks his wine. If he hears her, he doesn't care she's sitting next to him and whining about him.

"He did save your life, you know."

"That doesn't mean I have to marry him."

I reach to grab my own wine glass, but Beckett knocks my hand away. I may or may not be pregnant, so I shouldn't drink until I know. I need to take the test tonight. I need to know what my future holds.

I look at Rialta—my sister, in every way that matters. Lennox was the one who proposed marriage to Rialta. Vincent approved. After all, Lennox was the one who saved her, and ultimately, that's what Vincent cares about.

"If you don't want to marry Lennox, then you better find someone worthy of marriage in Vincent's eyes, or I don't see what choice you have," I say.

Rialta shoots daggers in his direction. "Don't worry, I will," she says.

I sigh and turn to Beckett. "We are going to have our hands full with Rialta for a while, I think."

He laughs. "Our lives would be boring without her."

"I'm boring, huh?" I raise my eyebrows, sliding my hand under the table to grab for his crotch.

"You, my queen, are anything but boring," he whispers.

But I'm not done with him. He doesn't get to make a comment like that without some punishment. I grab his cock, and he bites back a moan.

"Oh my god! Can you guys not at the table? Wasn't your show on the top deck enough?" Rialta asks.

Everyone rolls their eyes and groans when they realize what Rialta is insinuating.

Beckett and I laugh as I remove my hand.

"We never have enough," we say at the same time and look into each other's eyes, silently sending lust-filled promises of more broken furniture after this dinner. We are going to owe Kai and Enzo a fortune by the time we leave, but it'll be worth it.

For once, we can kiss and fuck like we have forever together, *but what's the fun in that?* Our impatient need to be together drives our lovemaking like time is running out, like we don't have forever and ever to love each other.

Although, forever is exactly what we have.

Thank you for reading Ri & Beckett's story! I hope you enjoyed it! Lennox's story is next!

One-click LENNOX Here

Rialta Corsi is the last woman I want to marry.
She's a prim princess, who doesn't belong in my world.
But I made a deal.
And I don't back out of my promises.
Even if the woman I agreed to marry drives me crazy,
I'll marry her.
But she's not ready to enter the world of Retribution Kings.

JOIN ELLA'S NEWSLETTER & NEVER MISS A SALE OR NEW RELEASE → ellamiles.com/freebooks

Love swag boxes & signed books?
SHOP MY STORE → store.ellamiles.com

ALSO BY ELLA MILES

LIES SERIES:

Lies We Share: A Prologue

Vicious Lies

Desperate Lies

Fated Lies

Cruel Lies

Dangerous Lies

Endless Lies

SINFUL TRUTHS:

Sinful Truth #1

Twisted Vow #2

Reckless Fall #3

Tangled Promise #4

Fallen Love #5

Broken Anchor #6

TRUTH OR LIES:

Taken by Lies #1

Betrayed by Truths #2

Trapped by Lies #3

Stolen by Truths #4

Possessed by Lies #5

Consumed by Truths #6

DIRTY SERIES:

Dirty Obsession

Dirty Addiction

Dirty Revenge

Dirty: The Complete Series

ALIGNED SERIES:

Aligned: Volume 1 (Free Series Starter)

Aligned: Volume 2

Aligned: Volume 3

Aligned: Volume 4

Aligned: The Complete Series Boxset

UNFORGIVABLE SERIES:

Heart of a Thief

Heart of a Liar

Heart of a Prick

Unforgivable: The Complete Series Boxset

MAYBE, DEFINITELY SERIES:

Maybe Yes

Maybe Never

Maybe Always

Definitely Yes

Definitely No

Definitely Forever

STANDALONES:

Pretend I'm Yours

Pretend We're Over

Finding Perfect

Savage Love

Too Much

Not Sorry

Hate Me or Love Me: An Enemies to Lovers Romance Collection

ABOUT THE AUTHOR

Ella Miles writes steamy romance, including everything from dark suspense romance that will leave you on the edge of your seat to contemporary romance that will leave you laughing out loud or crying. Most importantly, she wants you to feel everything her characters feel as you read.

Ella is currently living her own happily ever after near the Rocky Mountains with her high school sweetheart husband. Her heart is also taken by her goofy five year old black lab who is scared of everything, including her own shadow.

Ella is a USA Today Bestselling Author & Top 50 Bestselling Author.

Stalk Ella at:
www.ellamiles.com
ella@ellamiles.com

www.ingramcontent.com/pod-product-compliance
Lightning Source LLC
LaVergne TN
LVHW040052080526
838202LV00045B/3599